MW01094417

AMISH FOSTER GIRL

BOOK 2 AMISH FOSTER GIRLS (AMISH ROMANCE)

SAMANTHA PRICE

PRINT ISBN 978-1541027855

Print ISBN 978-1541027855

CHAPTER 1

Be of good courage, and he shall strengthen your heart,
all ye that hope in the Lord.
Psalm 31:24

STEPPING through the door of the café, Tara spotted Elizabeth waving at her from a table at the back.

Tara hurried over to her and slid into the chair opposite. "Sorry I'm late. You've finished your shift?"

"Jah. What kept you?" Elizabeth sipped her drink through a straw.

"Gretchen said William told her the horse was lame. I had to change over to Sox."

"Sox isn't good in traffic."

"He's a bit flighty. I'm glad Gretchen didn't know that, or I would've been stuck at home. This is my only day off this week apart from Sunday." Tara sighed and placed her bag down on the edge of the table. "I'm going to miss you so much when you get married. It'll only be me and Megan left at home."

"Gretchen and William might take in some more foster children."

"Really? Did they say that?"

Elizabeth laughed. "I don't know; it's not likely. They've only had the three of us for years."

"And with you gone, there'll be a spare room."

"True."

A young *Englisch* man came to take their order. Tara looked him up and down.

After he had taken their order and left, Tara leaned forward and whispered, "What's going on with that? Why did they hire a man? He's not even Amish."

Elizabeth shrugged her shoulders. "I don't know. I think they're going to make him a shift manager or something."

"What about you?"

"I don't care. I'm only here for the money. I'm not here to make a career out of it."

"Yeah, I guess so. Especially when you're getting married."

When the young man returned with Tara's tea, he picked up her bag and placed it on a chair before walking away.

Tara's mouth opened in shock at the man. "Did you see that?"

"What?"

"He touched my bag without even asking me."

"It's not a big deal. He just wanted to make more room on the table."

"I reckon it was weird. Would you have picked up someone's bag and moved it like that without asking?"

"Nee. I wouldn't. He didn't mean anything by it. Don't worry."

Tara poured her tea from the small teapot, filling the cup just as the man brought Elizabeth her coffee.

When he left, Tara leaned forward. "He doesn't have nice manners, either. He doesn't even smile."

Elizabeth groaned. "Stop being hung up about little things all the time."

"Well, don't you think that it was a weird thing to do—the thing about my bag?"

"Not especially. Don't over think things." Elizabeth ripped open a packet of sugar and poured it into her coffee. "Now, the reason I wanted you to meet me here was to talk about you minding the *haus* for me and Joseph."

"Oh, and I thought it was because you'd miss me so much when you're both away for a month."

Elizabeth smiled. "You know I will. I'll miss everyone."

"I'm still willing to mind your *haus.* I'm actually looking forward to being by myself."

"Jah, I remember you saying…"

"You've written down all the instructions, so I don't

forget anything, haven't you?" Maybe looking after Elizabeth's *haus* would pull her out of the doldrums.

"*Jah*, I've left a list on the kitchen table. I can't wait to move into it. Joseph's lived in it for three weeks and said there's a fair bit to do, but we can do things as we go, while we're living in it."

Tara frowned. "What things need doing?"

"Don't worry; the roof isn't going to fall in. There's nothing structural going on."

Tara watched her friend speak with excitement about her new life. It was still hard to believe that Elizabeth was getting married. She'd be someone's wife and have her own house just like a grown up.

Tara took a sip of tea. "Have you noticed how everything goes right for you, Elizabeth?"

"What do you mean?"

"Your birth family is rich and they want you to live with them and then there's Joseph. Your life is pretty much perfect. When you said you'd marry Joseph— boom, out of the blue, his family gets left a *haus* and they give it to Joseph."

Elizabeth laughed. "I guess so. *Gott* is watching over me."

"When you marry, I hope we can still meet up like this and do the simple things we used to do. You'll come back to the *haus* and visit us won't you?"

"*Jah*, that's where I grew up; it'll always be home."

Elizabeth had been with her foster parents, the Grabers, since she was eight, and then Tara and Megan

4

had joined them later. In the early years, there were various children coming for short stays, but none had stayed as long as the three girls.

Tara sighed. "I always thought I'd get married first, then you, and then Megan."

"I never really thought about it." Elizabeth brought the coffee cup up to her mouth, placed her perfect bow-shaped lips onto the rim of the cup and took a delicate sip.

"See? That's the difference between you and me. You never have to think about things; they just fall into place."

Elizabeth frowned and placed her cup back onto the saucer. "Tara, you have more attention from men than any other woman in the community. You've got nothing to grumble about."

"Yes, but the only man I want is Mark and he took off."

"You should've told him how you felt."

Tara raised her eyebrows. "If he'd loved me, he wouldn't have gone. Anyway, we told each other how we felt and I think that's what scared him off. I think if he'd stayed then things would've been different."

"He'll be back."

"We'll see. Anyway, enough about him. I'm trying to forget him."

"Okay."

"I'm looking forward to staying in your *haus.* It'll be a good distraction."

SAMANTHA PRICE

"Have you been pining after Mark?"

Shaking her head, she said, *"Nee.* Well, maybe a little, but don't you tell anyone."

"Who would I tell?"

"Aunt Gretchen, or Megan."

"I won't."

"It doesn't matter, I guess. Megan knows anyway and I'm sure she's sick of hearing me talk about him."

"I thought you were sneaking away to see someone for the last few months. I didn't know if it was one man or different men."

Tara giggled. "It was only Mark. We wanted to keep things quiet and I thought the relationship was going somewhere—heading toward marriage."

"I thought you might have been thinking of leaving the community. You told me I should move into the Doyles' home and not look back."

"Only because they're your family—your birth family—not because they're rich. It wouldn't have hurt to stay with them and get to know them."

"Their place wasn't my home. *Gott* had planned for me to be with the Grabers. They're always telling us we were sent to them for a reason and it's true." She stared into Tara's eyes. "Don't worry; he'll be back."

"I asked you not to talk about him. Can we change the subject?"

"Okay. What do you think of Joseph's *bruder,* Caleb?"

Tara shrugged her shoulders. "He's nice, I guess. I don't know him that well."

"I know that he likes you."

"How? Did Joseph tell you?"

Elizabeth smirked. "I can't say more."

Tara's attention was taken by a couple who sat down at the table next to them. She looked back at Elizabeth. "That's not fair. You've said that much, so you have to tell me more."

"Everything will work out for you just as things have worked out for me." Elizabeth wagged a finger. "Just you wait and see."

Tara nodded, not wanting to argue with her friend. The fact was that things had never worked out for her without her putting in a huge effort. Elizabeth had been the first of the three of them to get a job, and Tara had gotten one rejection after another until finally, she got the part time job at the quilting store. Megan had applied at a couple of places but, being painfully shy, she hadn't made a good impression in any of the job interviews.

"You've always been a good friend to me, Tara."

"Oh no. You're getting deep and meaningful on me."

Elizabeth laughed. "I'm going to miss everyone, that's all. My life's going to be so different once I'm married."

"I'm glad the three of us were together for the last few years. We're all different and none of that matters. In real families, people can be different too."

"Tara, I've never heard you talk like this."

Tara gave a sideways glance at the new waiter as he served the newcomers at the table next to them. Again with no smile, she noticed. She looked back at Elizabeth. "You're like my *schweschder,* and so is Megan. You just understand me a little better than she does."

Elizabeth narrowed her eyes. "You seem a little down. Where's the happy bubbly Tara?"

Tara inhaled deeply. "I've just been thinking about things that's all."

"About Mark?"

"You're not going to stop talking about him are you?"

"Well, is *he* the problem?"

Tara cringed. "Is it that obvious?"

"*Jah.* At least to me."

"I don't think I'll ever feel about anyone the way I felt about him." She glanced at Elizabeth and didn't want to ruin her happiness. "That's why I'm so excited to be looking after your *haus* until you get back." Tara felt better when the smile returned to Elizabeth's lips. She'd have to forget about her problems until after Elizabeth's wedding. Then, when she was by herself for that month, she could figure out what to do with the rest of her life.

"Are the Doyles coming to the wedding?"

"*Jah.* I've invited all of them."

"I can't wait to see them. You've described them all

so well. I want to see how closely the pictures in my head match up to how they look in real life."

"I hope they all come. I'm not so sure they will."

"Your birth mother and father will at least come, won't they?"

"They said they would."

"How do you feel about them now?"

Elizabeth shrugged her shoulders. "It still feels weird. I'm getting used to them being my family and Lyle Junior being the Simpson's real child. I'm used to thinking of *Mamm* Gretchen, *Dat* William, Megan, and you as my family."

"I'm sorry. I shouldn't have asked. I don't want to make you sad."

"I'm not sad. It's weird; that's all."

Tara didn't know anything about her birth parents, even whether they were alive or dead.

Tara said, "I guess it would feel weird to grow up thinking your parents were the people who raised you, and then find out they were someone else."

Elizabeth stared into her coffee. "Let's move on."

Tara laughed to ease the tension about the subjects that they wanted to avoid. It was clear that Elizabeth's wounds were still there, like her own.

"What would you like to talk about?" Tara asked.

"Caleb."

Tara tipped her head to one side. "I'm sensing some kind of a set-up."

Elizabeth raised her eyebrows and smirked again, causing Tara to sigh.

"Who put you up to talking to me about him?" Tara asked.

"You're not supposed to know."

"Of course I'm not. I'm not about to blab, so tell me."

"Joseph asked me to find out if you're interested in Caleb. Because Caleb likes you."

"I don't know how I feel about him. I don't know him very well."

"My wedding will be the perfect place to get to know him. He might make you forget all about the person I'm not allowed to mention."

"I hope so."

"Caleb is quiet, but he's worth taking the time to get to know."

"Well, forgetting about that certain person would be good. That's something I need to do, but I don't know if I should use another man to do it."

"Don't be silly. That's not what I meant. Wait a minute, though, it's not a bad idea."

Tara frowned until Elizabeth reached over and tickled her ribs, and then Tara had to join with Elizabeth's giggles.

CHAPTER 2

*Be thou my strong habitation, whereunto I may continually
resort: thou hast given commandment to save me; for thou
art my rock and my fortress.*
Psalm 71:3

ELIZABETH AND JOSEPH'S wedding was to be held at the
Grabers' house and the girls had spent the last week
scrubbing the house from top to bottom in readiness.
Because the house wasn't large, an annex had been set
up outside the kitchen to manage the food preparation
for the hundreds of guests. There were no formal invi-
tations sent out. The wedding was announced and
written up in the Amish newspapers, as was customary,
and people always showed up—usually in the
hundreds. Weddings were major social events for the

Amish and, for the young people, one of the best places to meet their future spouses.

On the morning of Elizabeth's wedding, Tara woke early. As soon as she had dressed, she bounded into Elizabeth's room and jumped on her bed.

"Wake up, sleepy head. This is the last morning you're going to be here. You'll be an old married woman by the end of the day."

Elizabeth opened one eye and then rolled over the other way, burying her face in the pillow. She'd never been an early riser.

"How come you're not excited?" Tara pulled the blankets off her friend and Elizabeth tried her best to grab them back.

Elizabeth sat up. "How early is it?"

"It's not early; it's time to get up. Aunt Gretchen is already awake. I can hear her downstairs."

Groaning, Elizabeth wiped her eyes. "I guess I should get out of bed."

"*Jah*, we've got so much to do yet today before people arrive. Starting with putting clean sheets on this bed, since it won't be yours after today."

The wedding was at nine o'clock. And now it was five thirty, only a few short hours before everyone arrived.

Tara leaped off the bed, and the two of them quickly remade it with clean linens. Then Tara unhooked Elizabeth's blue wedding dress from the peg behind the door.

"I'll put that on at the last minute, so I don't get it dirty."

"Good idea." Tara spread it over the bed.

All the women in their family, Aunt Gretchen, Megan, Elizabeth and Tara, had sewed the dresses for the attendants and the wedding dress for Tara. They'd also sewed the suits for Joseph and his two attendants.

Lastly, Tara placed the white organza prayer *kapp* and apron alongside the blue dress.

"Let's go and have breakfast before Aunt Gretchen finds a million things for us to do."

Elizabeth giggled while she changed into an everyday dress. Before they left the bedroom, Elizabeth wound her hair on her head and placed a prayer *kapp* on top.

When they reached the kitchen, they found a frazzled-looking Aunt Gretchen, and Megan making the breakfast.

"What's the matter?" Elizabeth said striding toward Gretchen.

"I've got a crowd coming and I'm feeling a little daunted." She pulled out a handkerchief and dabbed at her eyes.

Tara knew the truth of it was that she was sad that Elizabeth was leaving her. Elizabeth glanced up at Tara and, from the look on her face, Elizabeth also knew what the real problem was.

Elizabeth placed her arm around Gretchen. "We'll

handle it, *Mamm* Gretchen. Many of the ladies always help."

Gretchen nodded as Tara sat down at the table. "I know the real reason you're upset is that I'll be gone for a month looking after Elizabeth's *haus*."

That made Gretchen giggle. "It might be a *gut* rest for me."

Tara gave an exaggerated gasp. "Aunt Gretchen! I'm offended."

The four of them laughed.

Tara called her foster mother either Aunt Gretchen or *Mamm* Gretchen depending what mood she was in.

"We'll be alone for a whole month, *Mamm.* Just you me and *Dat.*"

Gretchen nodded at Megan's words. Megan was a homebody who was quite content to stay at home, cooking and sewing. She was also the only one out of the three of them to start right out calling William and Gretchen Graber, "*Mamm*" and "*Dat.*"

"You were such a sweet girl when you came to us, Elizabeth," Gretchen said, confirming Tara's thoughts of what she was upset about.

"Aren't I still sweet?"

Gretchen patted her hand. "You are. We'll miss you. It won't be the same with you gone."

"But we know how happy you'll be with Joseph. And you'll have lots of babies and bring them here for their *Gossmammi* Gretchen to babysit," Tara said.

"*Jah,* please," Gretchen said.

"That's a little too far in the distance. Let me think about getting married first before you start seeing me with babies," Elizabeth said.

"Everyone want pancakes?" Megan asked.

"Jah!" the women chorused.

"A man can't sleep in with women cackling," William said with a grin as he walked into the kitchen.

"You can't sleep in today," Tara said.

"We've still got so many things to do before people get here," Gretchen added.

William sat down next to Tara.

"Pancakes, *Dat?"* Megan asked.

"Jah, please." He turned to his wife. "I've got the men coming with the wagon at seven to move the furniture out to the barn and the benches into the house."

There was excitement in the air and Tara couldn't help feeling envious of Elizabeth. Everything always went her way. She was beautiful, her birth family was rich and they had wanted her to live with them. Now, she had a wonderful man who'd fallen deeply in love with her.

The next few hours past by in a blur as people rushed around inside the house. Finally it was time for Megan and Tara to go and help Elizabeth get dressed.

Elizabeth sat down on her old bed after pulling on her wedding dress.

She put her hand on her stomach. "I'm nervous."

Megan said, "You'll remember this day for the rest of your life, Elizabeth."

Elizabeth nodded.

Tara ran to the window to see more people arriving. The row of buggies was now so long it nearly reached the front gates. She looked down at a crowd of men, hoping Mark would be amongst them. Surely if he'd ever had real feelings for her, he'd be at her best friend's wedding. He knew how close she was to Elizabeth, and besides that, Joseph was one of his good friends.

Tara pushed him out of her mind and turned around to Elizabeth. "You look beautiful."

"Do I?"

"*Jah,* you always look beautiful, but especially today."

"*Denke,* Tara. Can you see any cars out there? What if they don't come?" Elizabeth asked, referring to her birth family.

"They'll come. They said they would."

Elizabeth pushed her bottom lip out slightly. "Can you look outside again?"

Tara moved back toward the window and looked down the driveway. "There are two cars coming through the gates now. That has to be them." Tara whipped her head around in time to see Elizabeth's smile.

"I'm glad they're here."

It amazed Tara that Elizabeth had been so quick to forgive her mother after what she'd done. Her birth mother had swapped her for a boy and had paid the boy's birth mother a lot of money. No one had known about her deception until Elizabeth's birth father saw her at the café where she worked. After her birth father had done some digging into the past, the secret came out.

"I hope they brought the old granny with them after all you told me about her," Tara said.

Elizabeth and Megan giggled.

"*Jah*, we'll see if she's as unfriendly as you've told us," Megan said.

"If she's here, you'll see I wasn't exaggerating. She looks at me as though I've got a secret and she's trying to uncover it."

Megan giggled. "Maybe she thinks you're not really her granddaughter."

"I'm sure that's it, but they're the ones who found me. I didn't go looking for them."

"That's only because you didn't know they existed," Tara pointed out.

"Yeah. That's what I mean. It's all so complicated in that family. I prefer to have a simple life like the one Joseph and I will have, and just have visits with them once in awhile."

Tara sighed. "You'll have a *wunderbaar* life, Elizabeth."

"You're perfectly suited to Joseph. I hope I meet a nice man one day," Megan said.

"You have to talk with people, Megan. Get over your shyness," Elizabeth said.

Megan pouted. "I wish I was more like you, Tara. You're so brave. You could talk to anyone."

"And why not? Everyone is just flesh and blood, deep down. There's no one who's better than anyone else. You've just got to think more confidently about yourself and stop hiding away in this *haus.*"

Megan nodded.

"She will in time," Elizabeth said fiddling with the *kapp* in her hands. "You must take her out with you, Tara."

"Jah, I will, if she'll go with me."

Elizabeth whipped her head around to look at Megan.

"Okay. I will get out more," Megan said.

Elizabeth smiled. "Good."

Tara stared at Megan, not so sure about what she'd said. Today Tara would try to find a man to suit Megan and then she'd introduce the pair. Maybe a quiet man would suit her, as long as he wasn't also shy.

Megan sat on the bed behind Elizabeth and brushed her wavy hair until it was silky smooth. Elizabeth's hair fell way past her waist. It hadn't been cut in the ten years she'd been with the Amish. Megan braided it and pinned it up, and then Elizabeth put on the organza prayer *kapp.*

Once Elizabeth was fully dressed, Megan and Tara hugged her and then they went downstairs first. Megan and Tara took seats next to Gretchen, and they watched as Elizabeth walked down the stairs and greeted Joseph who was waiting for her at the bottom. It brought a tear to Tara's eye the way they looked at one another. The couple then walked to the front of the room where the bishop stood.

The deacon opened with prayer and then Gabe Hostetler sang a hymn in High German. After that, the bishop preached a lengthy sermon. It was the same kind of preaching that Tara had heard so many times before. She scanned the seated crowd and the people who were standing, and still there was no Mark. Before she looked back to the front, she felt someone looking at her. Focusing her gaze as she quickly scanned the crowd, she saw that it was Caleb.

She gave him a little smile when she recalled that Elizabeth had said that he liked her. Caleb wasn't handsome like his younger brother, Joseph. He had a pleasant face, but that was marred by a large scar down one side of his face. Mark was the only one who'd made her heart pitter-patter.

Everyone stood when the bishop pronounced the couple husband and wife. Since the late January day was cold, they couldn't eat in the yard and the benches had to be taken out and tables brought inside for the wedding feast.

As attendants, Megan and Tara sat with Elizabeth at the head wedding-table. Tara let Megan sit next to Elizabeth knowing it would make her feel that little bit more special. There was no use looking around for

Mark any longer; if he were coming, he would've been here by now.

Instead of thinking about Mark, Tara concentrated on enjoying the food in front of her. There was no better food than could be found at an Amish wedding. Her gaze traveled over the various roasted and simmered meats, coleslaws and other salads, and all sorts of roasted vegetables. Tara took her plate and started helping herself to her favorites, creamed celery, and bologna.

CHAPTER 3

Yea, though I walk through the valley of the shadow of death,
I will fear no evil: for thou art with me; thy rod and thy staff
they comfort me.
Psalm 23:4

JUST BEFORE JOSEPH and Elizabeth left the Grabers' place after the wedding celebration, Joseph handed Tara the key to the old house. Elizabeth and Joseph were going to spend their wedding night at Joseph's parents' house, and would leave in the early morning to begin their four weeks' travels to visit many of Joseph's relatives.

Tara was looking forward to staying in the old house and she'd make sure that they arrived home to a spic and span home. She would've loved to start on a vegetable garden for them, but it was the wrong time of year to plant.

"Caleb said he'd be happy to take you there tomorrow morning if that suits. Or, are you going to borrow one of William's buggies for the month?"

"Nee, I haven't asked him about that. To tell you the truth, I didn't even think about a buggy." Tara bit down on the inside of her lip, but relaxed a little when she remembered there was a telephone in a nearby shanty and she could get a taxi to and from work. *"Jah,* I'd appreciate it if Caleb could take me there tomorrow. Would it be in the morning?"

"If that suits," Joseph said.

"The earlier, the better."

"How about I have him collect you around nine?"

"That would be perfect." Tara could've had William or Gretchen take her, but figured there was no harm in getting to know Caleb a little better. Besides, Mark might be getting to know some other girl somewhere—wherever he was, so why shouldn't she see who else might be out there?

The rest of the night was filled with cleaning, after the hundreds of guests left. Some of the women had stayed on to help, but after they left there was still a mountain of work to do.

"You go to bed, *Mamm.* Tara and I can finish this," Megan said.

Gretchen frowned. *"Nee,* it's too much for just the two of you."

"We're fine. You go," Tara said.

"Are you certain?"

"Jah!" both Tara and Megan said firmly.

"Denke. I need to put my feet up, they're aching."

When she left the room, Tara sat down.

"Are you going to leave this all for me?" Megan asked.

"I just need a five minute break. You do, too. Let's sit down for a bit."

Megan took her hands out of the dishwater, shook off the suds and wiped her hands on a nearby hand towel before she too slumped into a chair.

"That was such a long day. And I thought the bishop would never finish that sermon. That's got to be his longest ever."

Megan giggled. "It was long."

"Why don't you come and stay at Elizabeth's *haus* with me?"

"I couldn't. *Mamm* would be alone."

"She'll have *Onkel* William."

"Nee, I couldn't." Megan stared at the table.

"It's getting so that you're hardly ever leaving the *haus.* You don't go to any of the singings, so how do you think you'll meet a man?"

"There were plenty of men here today."

"Did you talk to any of them?"

"I didn't see any that I liked the look of that much."

"I didn't like the look of Mark until I got talking to him. I mean I thought he was handsome, but I didn't think he was for me. There was just something about him that put me off him at first."

"Was Mark here? I thought he'd gone away."

Tara slumped further into her chair wishing she'd never brought up his name.

$\sim$

TARA HAD her bags packed the next morning, ready and waiting for Caleb to fetch her. She'd already said goodbye to William before he'd left for work.

As soon as Caleb's buggy appeared at the bottom of the drive, she ran to the kitchen. "He's here." She wrapped her arms around Gretchen and gave her a tight hug, and then did the same with Megan.

"You're not going across to the other side of the world, Tara," Gretchen said.

"I might as well be. I've never lived on my own before."

"Well, if you get hungry, we've always got plenty of food here."

"*Denke,* but I've got everything organized." She walked out the door to meet the buggy.

"Hello, Caleb." She climbed into the buggy.

"Those yours?" His head nodded toward the house.

She looked back and saw her bags. "Oh, sorry, I completely forgot them."

"Stay there." He leaped from the buggy, collected her bags and placed them in the back.

"Denke." She looked back at the house to see that Megan and Gretchen were now standing at the front door. When Caleb got back into the driver's seat, she waved to them. Gretchen was smiling, but Tara knew it wouldn't be long before the older woman shed a tear.

Now sitting beside Caleb, she could see his scars close up. One side of his face had a huge scar, and she'd just noticed that his hands had some long scars, too, that looked like they'd come from deep scratches. Perhaps having that deep scar on his face had made him keep away from people.

Noticing that Caleb had barely said a word, she thought she should strike up a conversation. "It was a good wedding yesterday."

"Jah, it was."

"Why didn't you want to stay in Joseph's *haus?"*

He glanced over at her and then looked back to the road. "I wasn't asked."

"Oh. Would you have wanted to if you had been asked?"

"Dunno."

It didn't seem that he liked her, despite what she'd been told. He wasn't making much of an effort to converse, at any rate. So much for her hopes of him taking her mind off Mark.

Deciding it was his turn to talk about something, she put everything out of her mind and looked at the partially melting snow. The sun seemed unusually strong for the early part of a January day.

For the first time in months, Tara found herself smiling for no particular reason. The winter sun and the fresh air flowed over her face in waves. The once-green fields were now covered with snow and the beauty of the wildflowers was replaced with the shimmering sparkles of snow as the sun danced on the surface.

She found comfort in the sound of Caleb's graceful black gelding clip-clopping his way down the road back to the old homestead. Maybe it was the prospect of having a whole month to herself and finally having a little independence from her foster family that had altered her mood.

A good twenty minutes passed in silence before they came to the house.

"Here we are," he said as he pulled the buggy up.

"Ah good."

"You got the key?" he asked, seeming to use as few words as possible.

"I do. Joseph gave it to me yesterday."

He gave a grunt from the back of his throat. It was becoming clear to her why he wasn't married. He needed a good lesson on how to relate to women. Her opinion of him improved slightly when he took her bags out of the back and placed them at the front door. At least he was polite.

Before he got back into the buggy, Tara fumbled with the key. "Are you going to come inside with me?" she called out.

"Do I need to?"

"Um. No. It's just that... no, don't worry." She glanced at the old house behind her and tried to stop her imagination from running away with her. It was just an old house, but if hauntings were real, then this place would've been perfect for one. It wasn't at all like the usual Amish farmhouse.

"Bye," he said just before he clicked his horse onward.

Tara looked down at the large black key in her hand, and then ambled to the front door. She pushed it into the keyhole and with one turn to the right the door creaked open. She waited a moment before she stepped inside. A waft of stale air met her nostrils and she wondered why she'd agreed to stay in the house. As she took small, reluctant steps further inside, the stale air was mixed with a definite smell of damp—perhaps even mold.

The first thing to do was get rid of the old stale air. After she'd gone around opening all the windows for some much needed fresh air, she pulled her bags into the house.

The old *haus* would have been grand in its day. The ceilings were high and the staircase was wider than the average, with a beautifully carved wooden bannister— quite unlike any Amish *haus* would have. From the decorative iron ceiling roses and cornices, it was clear that this *haus* was not built to be a home for an Amish person. Amish homes were much plainer, practical, with no fancy features.

As she walked around inspecting the house, she wondered what parts Elizabeth and Joseph would keep and what ones they'd replace.

When Tara walked toward the kitchen, she realized she would have to do something about buying food. There was only one thing for it; she'd have to walk down to the phone and call a taxi to take her to the nearest market.

It was nearing midday, and knowing the coming night would be cold, Tara went into the kitchen to see if it might have a wood stove or some other heating system so she would not have to light the huge fire in the living room. Tara knew better than to light a fire in an unknown fireplace; it could have a blocked or un-working chimney and the place could very well fill with dirty and dangerous black smoke. To her delight, there was a woodburning stove in the kitchen, rather than a gas stove.

"I may as well do it sooner rather than later," Tara said to herself aloud, regarding going to the store.

A quick look around in the kitchen told her she only needed to buy food, as pots and pans, utensils and plates were all there. Everything would need scrubbing, but she could do that when she came back.

Tara had so much work to do in the *haus* before Joseph and Elizabeth got back that she felt a little guilty doing something that was not in her tight schedule.

She knew she could not work every waking hour of the day, but she'd factored that in as well. She'd brought her needlework and she would work on that for an hour or so every night. Tara smiled to herself; she was glad to have the project of working on Elizabeth and Joseph's place.

Driving back in a taxi from the brief visit to the food store Tara was pleased it hadn't taken long. That was only because she'd hidden from old Mrs. Yoder, the local gossip. Tara had been about to head down an aisle in the store when she saw her and turned on her heel to get away from her. Thankfully, Mrs. Yoder hadn't see her, or they'd still be talking now.

As the taxi drove her back to the house, a buggy came into view. She didn't know who it could be and she didn't recognize the horse.

When the taxi came closer, she suddenly did recognize the tall bay horse with his broad blaze. He was named Big and the owner, although he was nowhere in sight, was none other than Mark Young—the same Mark Young who'd run out on her.

"What the heck is he doing here?" she said under her breath.

"That'll be eight fifty, Ma'am."

She handed the driver a ten dollar bill. From her backseat position, she glanced at her reflection in the rear view mirror. Thankfully, she had no dark circles under her eyes from lack of sleep; she pinched her cheeks to give them color.

"There you go." The driver handed her the change.

After she had straightened her prayer *kapp* and tied up the loose strings, she grabbed hold of her two bags of groceries and stepped out of the taxi.

She knew that Mark and Joseph were friends, but wouldn't Mark know that Joseph wasn't here? And why hadn't he bothered to go to his good friend's wedding?

Tara walked around Mark's buggy and even looked inside it, but he wasn't there. Then she realized what was very wrong with this scene. The front door of the house was ajar, when she clearly remembered locking the doors and the windows before she left.

Now angry with him, firstly for leaving and secondly for arriving there the day after her best friend's wedding, she marched toward the house. With her arms full of shopping bags, she shoved the door wide open with her foot and walked through.

"Watch it!" The voice belonged to Mark.

Tara looked behind the door. "Mark Young!"

Mark stared at her and then raised himself from his crouched position, with hammer in hand. "Oh, it's you."

Suddenly feeling the weight of the bags, she set them by her feet. "Well?" She folded her arms and despite her feelings of rage for what he'd done to her, she wanted to reach out and touch him.

He flicked his dark hair away from his face and stared at her with his even darker eyes. Was he more muscled and a little taller, maybe?

"I could ask you the same question." His eyes ran up and down her in an instant and then their gaze locked in an intense stare.

Lifting her chin high, she announced, "I'm staying here while Joseph and Elizabeth are visiting." Tara unfolded her arms and clasped her hands in front of her.

"Joseph asked me to do some work on the place while he was away." He mirrored her earlier stance with arms folded across his chest.

"*Nee*, he wouldn't have. Not without telling me, and how did you get a key – do you even have one?"

He reached down to the floor and picked up a key. It was identical to the one Joseph had placed in her care.

Tara pouted. "I don't know why they wouldn't have told me that *you* would be coming here."

Mark shrugged his shoulders. "Looks like you'll have to put up with me coming and going all the time. Unless—"

CHAPTER 4

Be thou exalted, Lord, in thine own strength:
so will we sing and praise thy power.
Psalm 21:13

"Unless what?" Tara snapped back.

"I stay in the *haus* as well to save me the dr—"

"You'll do no such thing!"

Mark threw his head back and laughed. "You haven't changed."

"Neither have you!" It was lame, but that was all she could think to say. He had given her no apology and no reason why he'd left. He was acting like she was a total stranger instead of someone with whom he'd once talked of marriage. Didn't he feel he owed her a reason for leaving? Or was she so unimportant in his life that she was of no consequence to him?

"Well, we'll have to find some way of getting along together while I work on the *haus*."

She couldn't take it any longer; she had to know. "Why did you leave?"

He frowned at her. "What do you mean?"

"Forget it!" She picked up her two bags of groceries and stomped into the kitchen.

Tara was ashamed of herself. Ashamed that he could bring her to anger so quickly, and that he still had a place in her heart.

"Where are you off to now?" He followed her into the kitchen.

Annoyed at him shadowing her, she yelled over her shoulder, "You don't have to come with me. I'm just putting the groceries away."

"*Nee*. I'll do it for you." Mark hurried, overtaking her.

She ran in front of him. "I can do it."

He leaped in front of her again and stopped.

She had no choice but to stop and listen to him, as he said, "I'm here to help you."

"It's my food and I'm not cooking for *you*." She glared at him wanting him to leave her alone. He'd hurt her enough.

"I'll get the supplies in from the buggy."

"What supplies? You're not staying here! They said I could stay here and it's all been arranged."

"Relax! I'm not staying here, but I brought some food to eat while I'm here during the day working. I'll bring the things in when I put the horse away."

Horse away? How long is he staying for?

She turned to fill the teakettle with water and put it on the stove. A cup of hot tea would calm her jangled nerves and make her feel better.

SHE STOOD by the kitchen window, took a sip of freshly brewed peppermint tea and wondered whether it was any use her being there at all. Perhaps she should go home and let Mark keep an eye on the place. That would be better than seeing him all the time.

Tara cast her mind back over the past weeks since Mark had left.

When he came back into the kitchen with his food supplies, he looked at her groceries. "How long are you staying here? This doesn't look like four week's supply of food to me." He put his things on an open shelf.

She poured more boiling water into the teapot.

"I'll go to the store again. I'm not stranded here. I'll get a taxi like I did today." Mark stared at her without saying a word, so Tara continued, "I'm planning to be here until they get back. While we're on the subject, what work are you doing on the *haus*?"

"There are various things that need to be done."

Tara pulled out one of the wooden chairs from under the table and sat down. She poured herself a second cup of tea. "Help yourself to tea, if you wish." She would have him get his own tea if he wanted any.

"*Denke*, don't mind if I do."

While Mark poured tea, Tara took large sips from her cup, wishing she had added cold water to it. She would not make small talk with this man since he'd given her no apology for what he'd done. As soon as he sat at the table, Tara stood and poured the contents of her cup down the sink.

"Well, I don't have time to sit around all day; I've got things to do." Tara set about putting her groceries away in the utility room.

"I need to speak with you about something, Tara. Will you sit down?"

A large knot formed in Tara's stomach. Was she finally going to hear why he up and left her? Or was he just going to make suitable arrangements for the days ahead? Still in the utility room, she looked over her shoulder at him.

"What do you want to speak to me about?" By the way he sat rigidly looking at his cup; she could tell that he was in a serious mood.

"Just sit, will you?"

Tara let out a deep breath and decided she might as well get it over with. Whatever excuse he had, there was no way she'd ever forgive him for leaving without telling her. What he'd done brought back too many memories of the past. The right man for her would be a man who'd always be there for her no matter what. Her perfect man would make her feel safe, protected and loved.

"I want to speak to you about why I left suddenly."

She huffed. "Why does it have anything to do with me?"

"Don't be like that."

She stared into his dark eyes, wondering how they could be so cold and cruel when once he had been so tender and loving. "What makes you think I even care?"

"Because you did, and not so long ago. Before we left, you said—"

"Things have changed."

"All I want to do is talk."

She sighed noisily and sat down clasping her hands in front of her on the table. "I'm sitting."

He fixed his dark eyes on hers. "I was swept away with it all happening too quickly. My feelings for you have never changed. It was just that it was—well, I didn't know if marriage was for me."

She didn't buy his excuse. "Every Amish person wants to get married."

"You see? That's what everyone keeps saying, but what if it's not for me and I found that out later after we had married? I didn't want us both to be miserable."

"Now we don't have to worry about that." She bounded to her feet. "Like I said, I've got things to do." She hurried back to the utility room to unpack her shopping bags.

He stuck his head around the doorway. "I'll get back to work since you don't want to talk."

She didn't answer or turn around and when she heard him walk away, she glanced over her shoulder to make sure he'd gone. What he'd said was lame. If he'd been scared, why hadn't he discussed it with her at the time? He was the one who'd brought up marriage. Now she had to be stuck with him hanging around the house when she wanted nothing more than to be by herself.

Once she'd finished unpacking the food onto the shelves, she headed upstairs to the bedrooms. She decided on a small bedroom that overlooked the road so she could see who was coming and going.

"This will do nicely," she murmured to herself. She pulled off the older sheets on the single bed and replaced them with new clean sheets that she had brought with her. Once the bed was made, she opened the window to allow the chilly fresh air in.

She headed back downstairs to get Elizabeth's list. If she could get through everything as soon as possible, she could get back home.

Seeing Mark hammering something by the front door, she walked up to him and stopped in front of him, so he couldn't avoid seeing her. "How long will it take you to do these repairs?" She tapped the toe of her black boot impatiently.

He stopped what he was doing and looked up at her. "It's hard to say."

"Give me a rough estimate."

"Two weeks, maybe three."

She rolled her eyes and walked away. With Elizabeth's list in her hand, she sat down at the kitchen table.

She had to laugh when she read her friend's list.

Relax

Have a good time

Don't worry about anything

Enjoy some time alone

Don't do any work

Try not to miss me too much

Love,

Elizabeth

She'd been fooled into thinking she was there to help Elizabeth. She threw the list down on the table. Now she had a decision to make. And that was, should she stay there and ignore Mark the best she could, or go back home?

The repairs had to be done because that's what Joseph wanted, and she would stay there and clean the place so Elizabeth and Joseph would have a clean place to come home to. Mark Young would not ruin her plans. Tomorrow she had work at the quilting store, but as for the rest of the day, she'd clean the kitchen.

Hours later, she heard Mark call out, "I'm heading off now."

"Okay."

He stuck his head around the door. "Do you want me to bring anything back with me tomorrow?"

"I won't be here."

"Why not?"

"I work. Remember?" Immediately, she regretted her harsh tone.

"I've got the fire ready for you. The chimney's okay and all you have to do is light it."

"Denke." She cleared her throat and looked away from him. When she looked back around, he was gone.

Moving to the window, she watched as he hitched his buggy, and kept watching as Big trotted away from the house.

That night, she cooked herself an easy dinner and after that, she settled in front of the fire with her needlework. As far as she could, she put all thoughts of Mark out of her mind.

CHAPTER 5

While the earth remaineth, seedtime and harvest, and cold and heat, and summer and winter, and day and night shall not cease.
Genesis 8:22

In a different part of town.

IT WAS three weeks after he'd buried his wife, and Redmond O'Donnell decided it was time to sort out her belongings. He could no longer bear to look at his wife's clothes and her bits and bobs. The loss was difficult enough without these constant reminders. He didn't want to do it alone, but neither did he want to put his son or his daughter through the task.

His wife had suffered from heart disease and had been sick for some time. It was the pneumonia she'd caught in her last days that escalated her illness to the point she could no longer continue. They'd all three been there with Marjorie when she passed away—their thirteen year old daughter, Avalon, and his son from his first marriage, Brandon. Marjorie had clutched his hands and mumbled something about being sorry and the rest of her words made no sense. Those words had been her last.

He walked into their once-shared wardrobe to start packing her clothing. Everything was to go except for her jewelry and a few keepsakes to pass on to Avalon. He took armfuls of her clothes and placed them on the bed for Goodwill.

Blinking back tears, he recalled when he'd had to do the exact same thing when Brandon's mother had died. It didn't seem fair that he'd had two wives and they'd both died before him.

A rare shade of turquoise blue caught his eye as it peeped through the black that had become Marjorie's main color choice for clothing. He pulled on the material and out came Marjorie's favorite dress she wore on vacations. Pushing his face into the dress he breathed in Marjorie's favorite scent that lingered in the fabric.

Reminding himself to be practical, he placed the dress back on the pile with the rest of her clothes. There was no point keeping her outfits even if they held memories.

Redmond continued the task, amazed how women thought they needed so many clothes. He had less than a tenth of the clothing Marjorie had. Many of these items were unworn, with their price tags still attached. It seemed wasteful to him, but Marjorie and he had different views on most things. Theirs had been an attraction of opposites.

Once all the clothing items that had been on hangers were on the bed to be packed in boxes, he turned his attention upward to Marjorie's shelves. Seeing a large box, he walked over and pulled it down. After he'd placed it on the bed, he blew off a fine layer of dust, and then opened the lid. Inside was Marjorie's fine lace wedding dress that she'd worn a good twenty years ago. He replaced the lid quickly. The decision was simple. Avalon might like to wear her mother's dress on her wedding day.

He put the box on the far side of the room, which he'd designated as the 'keeper side.'

The next task was her shoes, and dozens upon dozens of pairs went into large boxes. He scratched his head, knowing that he'd set himself a task that would take days, not hours, and he was going to need a lot more boxes.

Noticing a red box at the back of the shelf Marjorie's wedding dress box had been on, he took it down and saw that it was full of jewelry. Avalon could have the task of going through this box. She'd know the pieces of value and the ones that were merely costume jewelry since she'd always gone shopping with her mother. The box was placed beside the wedding dress.

He stood on tiptoes, and then headed back near the door so he could see if there was anything else on the top shelf. On tiptoes again, he saw that there was something else; another box. Reaching up, he could just get hold of it and he tried to keep it steady. He overbalanced and the box tipped to one side and out scattered a mass of papers. Looking at the mess on the floor, he recognized them as important documents and receipts. Most of them looked aged. Sitting down with his legs in front of him, he took hold of his glasses that he'd folded over the top edge of his shirt and placed them on the bridge of his nose. Stubbornly, he refused to wear his glasses unless it was absolutely necessary, but knowing official documents were never in large print, it was a fitting occasion to wear them.

The box had contained their certificate of marriage and the birth certificates of Avalon and Brandon. There were also receipts for the major purchases they'd made over the years. He reached out for the next one and adjusted the distance from his face, so he could read the small print with his bifocals. His heart pounded as he read, and then re-read the document.

"How can this be true? It can't be!"

Sadness mixed with regret pained his heart as though he'd been stabbed repeatedly with a dagger. The paper fell from his hands and he doubled over closing his eyes. Marjorie's last words echoed in his head. Her words finally made sense.

CHAPTER 6

And we know that in all things God works for the good of those who love him, who have been called according to his purpose.
Romans 8:28

AT EIGHT THE NEXT MORNING, Tara was hurrying up the road to get a taxi. She noticed a buggy coming toward her and recognized it as belonging to Caleb. He gave her a wave and then pulled his buggy over.

"Where are you headed?"

She walked right up to him. "I've got work today."

"And you're walking there?" His eyebrows drew together.

"Nee. I'm heading to call the taxi."

"Don't you work at the quilting store in town?"

She smiled at him. "That's right."

"I can drive you there."

"Really?"

He offered a friendly smile. "Yeah, jump in."

Once she was sitting next to him, she asked, "What are you doing out this way?"

"Joseph asked me to keep an eye on you."

"Did he?"

Caleb nodded.

"I wonder why."

Caleb laughed.

"What's funny?" she asked.

"Nothing."

He was much friendlier than he'd been the previous day.

"Tell me."

He glanced at her. "It's nothing. I'm laughing at myself for asking you dumb questions."

"Oh. What questions?"

He glanced at her with a twinkle in his eyes. "When I asked if you were walking to work."

"Well, I could've been."

He looked back at the road. "Not in this weather."

"I'm just trying to make you feel better," Tara said with a giggle.

He glanced at her again, smiling. "I'm too far gone for that."

"What kind of work do you do?"

"I work on the family farm, but I'd rather be a builder like Joseph."

"Can't you do that? Joseph is younger, isn't he?" Joseph had so many brothers it was hard to know who was older than whom.

"The older sons work on the farm, the younger ones get to do whatever they want, it seems."

"You're not working on the farm now?"

He frowned at her. "Harvest is finished."

"Oh, silly me. You're not alone in the 'dumb question' department!"

He gave a quick laugh. "We're repairing the barn and fixing the wagons, and things like that. At this time of year, there's not much else to do."

Soon they were in town and as she stepped out of his buggy, she said, "*Denke,* Caleb."

"Will you be okay to get home? I can come and get you."

"*Nee,* that's fine. I'm not sure what time I'm finishing today anyway."

"I'll need to check on you every couple of days to keep Joseph happy. I hope you don't mind."

Tara smiled. "Okay. I don't mind at all."

When he drove away, she headed toward the quilt store. She glanced back to see how far Caleb's buggy had gotten when she saw Mark's buggy heading toward her. She whipped her head away, so he wouldn't know she'd seen him. In the reflection from a nearby window, she saw a young woman beside him. Jealousy mixed with rage inside her. Had he been trying to get back in her good books while also dating someone else? Is that why he'd wanted to keep their relationship quiet from the start? A dozen scenarios flashed through her head before she pushed the door of the quilt store open.

~

WHEN TARA WAS SITTING down to eat dinner that night, she heard a buggy. She jumped out of her chair and rushed to the window. It was William and Gretchen. After she had pushed her plate in the oven to keep it warm, she headed out to meet them, hoping nothing was wrong.

Gretchen walked over to her when she climbed out of the buggy and Tara searched her face to see what her mood was.

"Is everything alright?"

"*Jah*, but we've got some news."

Tara frowned. "Good or bad?" In her experience, news coming out of nowhere was normally bad.

"Let's sit down and we'll tell you."

When they were all seated in the living room, Gretchen began, "Carol came around earlier today."

The only 'Carol' Tara knew was Carol Booth, her caseworker. "Why? She said she's finished with the visits because I'm over eighteen."

"There's someone who's tracked you down."

"A relative?"

Gretchen nodded. "Your mother's brother."

"Oh. Where's he been?"

"I don't know the full story. He wants to meet you. She didn't tell us too much."

William added, "Now that you're eighteen you're in charge of yourself, it seems."

"*Jah*, I'm an adult. Well, I'll call her and find out about him." If she'd had an uncle why hadn't he taken her in? She still didn't know anything about her parents, not even whether they were alive or dead. All she knew was that she was adopted as an infant; when she was around eight, she was relinquished by her adoptive parents; and then she was adopted again only to have the same thing happen. It seemed the only people who never gave up on her were Gretchen and William.

"You don't have to unless you want to," Gretchen said. "Anyway, you can learn more about him from Carol."

"It worked out well for Elizabeth. She's pleased to know who her real parents were."

Tara wondered if her uncle was rich, like Elizabeth's family who had appeared out of the blue. Somehow, she doubted it. Elizabeth was the one who had all the luck.

"You can learn something about your parents."

Tara shrugged. "I'm not sure I want to know." She didn't want to shock William and Gretchen by saying what was really on her mind. Her parents hadn't wanted her, so why would she want to know about them? "I wonder why after all this time he's come forward. Why now?"

"Most likely he didn't want to interrupt your childhood," Gretchen said.

"I guess. That could be a reason."

"There's one way to find out," William said.

"I'll call her tomorrow. I'm curious now. Have you seen the house yet?"

"Nee," Gretchen said looking around.

"Let's start in the kitchen."

Tara tried to remain herself while her foster parents were at the house, while inside she was struggling with the information they'd come with.

Fifteen minutes later, she was waving goodbye to Gretchen and William. Feeling a little strange being all alone again, she pulled her dinner out of the oven and sat down in front of it. After a few minutes of pushing her food around the plate with a fork she covered it over and put it away for later.

What if her uncle came with the offer of a new life just as Elizabeth's relatives had? Would she leave the Amish looking for a better life? If Mark had been a more reliable person they would've married and her choice would've been easy. Now, she had to keep her mind open.

She slumped into the couch and picked up her needlework. Looking over at the fire, which needed more logs, she wondered why Mark hadn't been there that day.

THE NEXT MORNING, she was more anxious than ever to find out more about her uncle. Before she called for her taxi, she made a call from the shanty to Carol.

After the exchange of pleasantries, Carol delivered some news.

"Tara, it's not your uncle. I told Gretchen and William it was an elderly male family member and they immediately started referring to him as your uncle. I just didn't correct them. Now that you're eighteen, I need to give such information directly to you."

"If it's not my uncle, who is it?"

"Your father. I was contacted by your birth father."

"He's alive?"

"Yes, very much alive. It's a long story, but he's anxious to meet you. He's only just learned of your existence."

"Oh." That was all Tara could say for a few moments.

"Tara, are you still there?"

"Yes. I'm trying to take it all in."

"I know this is a surprise. Would you like to meet him?"

"Does he want to meet me?"

"He's very anxious to meet you."

"What's he like?"

"I've only talked with him over the phone. He seems very nice."

"I'd like to meet him."

"I'll set up a meeting for the two of you. Call me back later this afternoon. By that time I should have something set up."

"Thank you, Carol."

Tara hung up the phone and wished she didn't have to go to work that day. An orphan was what she'd always assumed she was. It was easier to think she was an orphan rather than having people out there somewhere who hadn't wanted her.

She turned around when she heard the sounds of a buggy coming toward her. It was Caleb.

He pulled up next to her. "Want me to drive you to work?"

"Jah, denke." She climbed up beside him and he flicked the reins and the horse moved on.

He glanced over at her. "Are you alright?"

"I've just had the most bizarre news from my caseworker. I suppose you don't know what a caseworker is?"

"Of course, I do. What did they say?"

She shook her head, still not believing that she had a real live father after all this time. "She told me that my father is still alive and that he only just learned about me."

"How does that work?

Tara shrugged. "I've got no idea, but I'm going to

find out soon because, Carol, my caseworker, is setting up a time when we can meet each other."

"That's good. You can finally get some answers to the questions you've had."

"How do you know I had questions?"

"If I were in your position, I'd have a lot of questions. It's only natural."

"I hope he's not expecting someone perfect. He's probably built up an image of someone wonderful." Tara sighed.

"Tara, you *are* wonderful."

She narrowed her eyes at him thinking he might be joking. His face showed no hint of a smile.

He was too shy to talk much, and yet not too shy to say something so lovely to her. "You don't know a lot about me."

"If I found out I had a daughter, I'd be happy if she was exactly like you."

She could sense he was being genuine. "But you don't know anything about me."

"I've been watching you for some time." He laughed. "That came across as a bit creepy. I've kind of been observing you. I couldn't get to know you because you were close with someone else. I thought he'd gone, but it seems now he's back."

She didn't say anything, but she knew that he meant Mark.

"Well, that's over."

"Is it?"

He glanced over at her and she nodded. "It is."

"Why's he back? I'm sorry; it's none of my business. I'm always saying the wrong thing."

"I don't think you are. You don't say enough."

He laughed. "That's because whenever I say something I usually end up regretting it. It's better if I keep quiet."

"I don't think that's true. You should speak up all the time. Anyway, Mark's doing work on the house. He says Joseph asked him to do repairs before they got back."

"I see. That explains a few things." When he stopped the buggy, she saw that they had already reached the quilting store.

"There you are."

"Thanks for talking to me about my father. You made me feel much better."

He smiled at her. "Glad to be of help. Can I take you home tonight?"

"I finish at three."

"Then I'll be here at three."

"I'd like that." She stepped out of the buggy and hurried to her work.

DURING HER LUNCH BREAK, Tara called Carol. All morning long she'd been unable to get her father off her mind.

"I know you told me to ring later today, but I was wondering if you'd set up a time with him yet?"

"I did. I spoke to him right after our conversation this morning. He's very keen to meet you."

"When?" Tara asked.

"It's up to you. He said for you to name the time and the place and he'd be there."

"I think I'd like to meet him at home."

"At the Grabers'?"

"Yes. I think tomorrow night at seven."

"Okay. Are you sure things aren't moving too fast for you? You could write him a letter first."

"No. I want to meet him and hear from his own lips how I came to be adopted and fostered, and who my mother is."

"Okay. I'll arrange it."

"Thanks for everything, Carol."

"I'm glad to help out."

For the rest of the day, Tara tried to concentrate on her job but all she could think about was her father and what he would be like and what he would look like. She had so many questions. With his sudden appearance in her life and his curious claim about only recently learning about her, all of that gave her more questions.

When Caleb came at three o'clock, she was anxious to share her news.

"Caleb, I'm going to meet my father tomorrow night."

"Things are moving quickly."

"I know. Would it be too much trouble for you to drive me to Gretchen's, so I can ask her if it's okay to meet there tomorrow night? I arranged it for seven o'clock."

"That's fine. I can drive you there now."

"Thank you. And then wait for me and then take me back to Joseph and Elizabeth's?"

He nodded. "Okay. It's probably a good idea to meet him at the place where you feel most comfortable."

"That's what I thought. My whole life I didn't know anything about my parents, not even whether they were living or not. Now I found out my father is alive, and tomorrow I'll find out about my mother."

"Do you know anything about her at all?"

She shook her head. "I still don't even know whether she's alive or dead. The main thing I want to know is why she gave me away."

They drove for awhile in silence. When they arrived, she invited him into the *haus*, but Caleb told her he'd prefer to wait in the buggy.

After she'd told Gretchen that she'd arranged to meet her birth father, Gretchen agreed for the meeting to take place in their home. Because Caleb was waiting in the buggy, she took some cookies that Megan had just baked and headed back out to him.

"How did it go?" Caleb asked.

Climbing up next to him, she said, "Good, and I scored us some cookies." Once she was seated, she handed him two and kept two for herself.

He smiled as he took them from her. "Are these chocolate chip?"

"Looks like it. "

"They're my favorite. I love chocolate." He took a bite and smiled his approval before he turned the buggy around and headed back to the road.

CHAPTER 7

And be not conformed to this world: but be ye transformed
by the renewing of your mind, that ye may prove what is
that good, and acceptable, and perfect, will of God.
Romans 12:2

TARA JUMPED down from Caleb's buggy when they
arrived back at the house. *"Denke,* Caleb. "

"I can do the same again tomorrow."

"That won't be necessary, *denke.* I have the day off
tomorrow."

"Okay. I hope all goes well with meeting your
father. "

"So do I."

"I'll see you later, Tara. If you need anything, just
give me a yell."

"I will." She headed to the house, more impressed by Caleb every moment she spent with him. He had a quiet self-confidence hidden beneath his initial shy exterior.

She wasn't home long when she heard a buggy. Looking out the window, she saw Mark's tall bay horse, Big, heading toward the house.

"Aargh! Why couldn't he have done his work when I was out today?" She poured herself a cup of tea, disappointed that her peace would now be ruined by Mark's loud hammering.

He knocked on the door and when she opened it, all she could see was a bunch of flowers. He lowered them and a smile lit up his handsome face.

She hid her delight at being given flowers. "What are those for?"

"Don't you mean 'Who are these for?' instead?"

She put one hand on her hip. *"Nee,* I meant, 'Why?'"

"A peace offering."

"For me?"

He held them out toward her. *"Jah."*

She reached out and took the flowers. "Peace is a good thing. Are you coming inside?"

"I can't do the repairs on the house from the outside."

She stepped aside, allowing him to pass, and remembering her manners, added, *"Denke* for the flowers."

"I'm glad you like them. They're not easy to find at this time of year."

She was confused by his comment. The mixture of roses, daisies and lilies were obviously store-bought flowers and not ones picked by the roadside. If she mentioned her thoughts, however, he would accuse her of being argumentative. She kept quiet.

"How about a cup of tea?"

"Okay."

She placed the flowers down beside the sink and poured him a cup of tea.

She'd made a full pot, planning on having more than one while she planned out the rest of her day. Once she placed his cup on the table, she set about finding a vase for the flowers. All she could find was a large preserving jar. She'd have to look for a nice vase in town to leave as a gift to Elizabeth.

When she'd arranged them nicely, she pushed the flowers into the center of the table.

"They look pretty."

"They do." She sat down to drink her hot tea.

"How was work today?"

"It was fine."

"I know you hate me for leaving when I did, without a word, and I know I was wrong, but if we can't go back to being how we were, can we at least be friends?"

"I don't know if we can be friends. I need to be able to trust all my friends."

"I figured out that it's your past making you act like this."

"Forget my past. This has nothing to do with people letting me down before. And it's not an excuse for you to let me down."

"Now come on, Tara. That's going a bit too far."

She bit her lip. Too often she said what was on her mind without thinking her words through. "What I mean is that you were talking of marriage and we were imagining a future together. We were even talking about names for our *kinner,* and the next thing I know, you just run off without a word. You deserted me. And then you come back as if nothing has happened." Glaring at him, she added, "It's not okay."

"You didn't let me explain."

"There's nothing to explain."

"It's not all about you all the time, Tara. I'm a real person and I have feelings too. And I know you're spending time with Caleb just to get back at me. That's your way of punishing me and it's a juvenile thing to do. You can't build the man's hopes up like that."

Tara laughed. "That's the silliest thing I've ever heard."

"That's the only reason I can think that you even talk to him. He never says two words, so I doubt that the two of you could find anything in common."

"We talk about many things. He says a lot to me."

"I don't want to argue with you, Tara."

"It appears you do. You say silly things and when I

set you straight you don't listen, you say you don't want to argue." Tara shook her head and then took a sip of tea.

"I realized when I came back and you were so mean to me that you have a fear of people leaving you just like your parents left you. I've a friend studying psychology and I discussed it with him. You have a fear of abandonment."

She screwed up her face. "You don't know anything about my feelings or my fears. Or my parents and what happened with them, so leave that topic alone."

He sighed. "Can't things go back to the way they used to be? I just want you to know that I was scared to make the next move—marriage—but I'm over that now."

"The moment has past."

"You can't mean that."

"I thought you were reliable and a strong-minded man. On the outside, you're handsome and strong, but on the inside you're a five-year-old boy."

"They say every man needs a woman to help him mature."

"Who says that?"

He shrugged. "You know—'they,' whoever that is."

"I want someone who knows me and knows himself. Maybe I won't marry; maybe after tomorrow night I'll have a new life and I'll leave the community for good."

"What do you mean after tomorrow night?"

"If you must know, I'm meeting my birth father."

Delight spread over his face. "Tara, that's fantastic. Have you spoken to him on the phone?"

"I'm meeting him for the first time tomorrow and we haven't spoken before at all." She shook her head. "I don't know what he'll say, or whether it will be good or bad. Maybe he'll want me to move in with him and his family, just like Elizabeth's parents wanted. Maybe once we meet, he'll want to have no more to do with me. I won't know until after tomorrow night."

"It's possible, either way." He drank the rest of his tea in silence. *"Denke* for the tea. I had better go do some jobs while I'm here."

CHAPTER 8

If we confess our sins, he is faithful and just to forgive
us our sins, and to cleanse us from all unrighteousness.
1 John 1:9

REDMOND O'DONNELL KEPT the news to himself that
Marjorie and he'd had another child, saying nothing to
Avalon or Brandon. He had no idea how this young
woman would take the news he had to tell her. He only
hoped that she wouldn't hate him and his late wife. The
worst thing would be to find out that she'd had a
miserable life. Wiping a tear from his eye, he wished
things would've been different. Long ago, he'd learned
that life takes twists and turns, and he had to cope with
whatever was thrown at him. With his first wife dying

and now losing his second wife, Marjorie, he'd had his share of sorrow.

Brandon lived away from home and had done so for some time. He called a sitter to watch Avalon while he was out. She was kind of old for that, but he hated to leave her home by herself at night. He told Avalon he had a business appointment after dinner, knowing she wouldn't ask questions.

Picking up his wife's photo on the nightstand, he wrestled with feelings of guilt. Surely there had been signs that he'd missed. If he'd been a more sensitive and caring person, he would've picked up on those signs.

"We're both to blame," he said as he put the photo back where it had been.

He took hold of his car keys, a small photo of Marjorie, along with the birth certificate, and headed off to the address that the social worker had given him.

"WHERE DO you want us to go?" William asked Tara.

"I guess I'll talk to him myself in the living room if you want to stay in the kitchen. If all goes well, I'll call you out to meet him."

"Oh, I hope it goes well," Megan said.

"We all do. Just don't leave us," Gretchen said, now giving Tara a hug.

Tara said, "I'm not going anywhere."

WHEN THEY HEARD a car's engine outside, Gretchen said, "That's gotta be him. We'll be praying for you, Tara."

And then Tara was alone in the living room. Her heart was pounding. This was unquestionably the most nervous she'd been in her life. She was anxious to hear what the man had to say but at the same time, she hoped he wasn't expecting someone wonderful. She peeked out the window to see a tall man who easily had to be as old as her foster father.

He had gray hair, was clean-shaven and wore a brown suit—a business suit.

When he knocked on the door, Tara took a deep breath and then opened it. The man smiled when he saw her and then his mouth turned down at the corners and his lips quivered a little, as though he was about to cry.

Should she hug him, kiss him, or shake his hand? What was appropriate? She offered her hand, thinking that was the safest option at this point. "I'm Tara."

"And I'm Redmond O'Donnell."

"Come in. We can sit over here." He followed her to the couch and they sat down.

"Thank you for meeting me."

"Can I call you Redmond?"

"Yes. Please do."

"Carol said you didn't know anything about me. How did you find out about me and when did you find out about me?"

"My wife and your birth mother, Marjorie, died recently."

Tara's fingertips flew to her throat. Her mother was dead! Now that she knew that for certain, she was filled with sorrow for the lost opportunities. She'd never meet her. Tears filled her eyes.

"I'm sorry. I don't mean to make you sad," he said.

"I don't think there's any avoiding it. Please go on. I have to know."

"It wasn't until I was clearing out my wife's things that I came across your adoption papers." He stopped, closed his eyes and pinched the bridge of his nose. "I should start at the beginning. My wife and I were total opposites, which led to frequent clashes particularly when we were first married. We disagreed on almost every subject. Finally, when she thought she couldn't take any more of me, she left me and Brandon, my young son from my first marriage. I was already a widower when I met Marjorie. For the first few days after Marjorie left, I was angry, but then I tried to find her. A year later, I found her and convinced her to come home."

"And she'd had me within that year?"

Redmond nodded.

"Why didn't she contact you and tell you about me?"

He shook his head. "The only clue I have about that is the last words she uttered from her hospital bed. Her words didn't make sense then, but when I found your adoption papers, they clicked."

Tara leaned forward wanting to know everything.

"She said, *Tell her I'm sorry, but it was too late. It had already been done and there was nothing I could do.* Then she took her last breath."

"Was she talking about me?" Tara blinked back more tears that filled her eyes. Her mother *had* cared about her.

"There was nothing else she could've been talking about. She knew I'd find those papers. She would've known I'd stop at nothing to find you. Going by the date of your birth, you'd been adopted. Keeping quiet would've been Marjorie's way to save everyone pain."

"I had no idea. I never knew anything."

"I can only assume she didn't want me to have the pain of knowing that our first-born child wasn't with us." He wiped away a tear. "We went on to have a daughter."

"You did? So, she'd be my—"

"Sister. And you have a half brother, Brandon. Your sister's name is Avalon. She's just turned thirteen."

Tara sat there, stunned. She had a sister and a half brother. "Do they want to meet me?"

"I wanted to meet you first before I mention you to them. I didn't know if you'd want to meet them and I didn't want you to be overwhelmed. I don't know how they'll take it when they find out their mother kept this secret from all of us."

"I grew up not even knowing if my parents were alive or dead and what the circumstances were. I'm just grateful to know how I came to be born and to know that I'm not alive under bad circumstances. I would like to meet Avalon and Brandon as long as they want to meet me."

His face lit up. "You would?"

"Yes. Did Carol tell you anything about me or my past?"

"She didn't."

Tara went on to tell him about the two families she'd been in, and finishing by telling him about the happy ending, that she'd landed on her feet with the Grabers. "Do you want to meet them?"

"I'd love to."

Tara sprang to her feet and ran into the kitchen. Seeing their faces staring at her awaiting instructions, she waved them forward.

"Come on. He wants to meet you guys."

Tara led them out to Redmond and made the introductions.

After an awkward beginning, William told Redmond some stories about Tara when she'd first come to them.

"She was a lovely girl," Gretchen insisted frowning at her husband.

"She's always been lovely," William said, "but she's always had a strong mind to do things her way. There were a few times she tested us."

"Both my wife and I were strong minded people. Sometimes to our detriment, I'm afraid. I was just telling Tara about our rocky marriage in the beginning years before we learned to compromise and take the time to understand each other."

"I have a sister and a half brother," Tara announced proudly. "I hope they'll want to meet me."

"I'm sure they will." Redmond glanced at his wrist-watch. "I should be going."

Tara jumped to her feet. "We didn't give you tea or anything!"

"Yes, will you stay for some hot tea?" Gretchen asked.

He shook his head. "I should go." He looked over at Tara. "Perhaps after I tell my children, you might be able to come to my house? Maybe come for dinner with us?"

"I'd like that."

"Good." He handed her a card. "All my phone numbers are on that. We'll talk soon."

"I hope so."

Tara stood up to walk him to the door.

After Redmond had driven away, she turned back to look at the Grabers and Megan. They were all staring at her. She walked back and sat down with them.

"I never thought this day would come. I honestly thought my birth parents were dead. Now I know a little about my mother, and my father is alive, and I'm someone's sister. I even have a half brother."

"Don't forget us," Megan said.

"I won't! You're my family, silly. All of you are."

William and Gretchen smiled and looked lovingly at each other. Tara noticed that they hadn't felt threatened in the slightest by her father's appearance in her life. They were so full of love and so giving, they were happy because she was happy.

"Stay here tonight?" Megan asked.

"*Nee.* I've got all my things over there at the *haus.*"

"I'll take you back whenever you're ready," William said.

"*Denke.* I should go now before it gets too late."

"Come into the kitchen first," Megan said pulling Tara by the arm.

As soon as they were in the kitchen, Megan whispered, "What's going on with you and Mark?"

"Nothing."

"Have you seen him since he's been back?"

"Joseph has given him jobs to do at the *haus.* I can't tell you how annoyed I was about that. No one told me that was going to happen."

"I know how you feel about him, but—"

"Felt about him," Tara corrected her.

Megan nodded. "I saw him with Mary Lou."

Tara frowned at the news. Could it have been Mary Lou she'd seen in the buggy with him in town? "Where did you see them?"

"Yesterday at the markets. I went there with *Mamm.*"

"It might mean nothing."

Megan shook her head. "Okay, I didn't want to tell

you this today, but Mary Lou's *scheweschder,* Sue Anne, told me that they're secretly dating. I thought you should know. I'm sorry if it upsets you."

"That's hard to believe. He told me he wants to make things right between us and he's sorry for leaving the way he did." Tara held her head. So many things were happening.

"I don't know. What if he's lying?" Megan asked.

"Maybe Sue Anne was mistaken. Maybe Mary Lou just *wants* to be dating Mark."

"I guess it's possible."

"Denke for telling me, Megan."

"I thought you should know. Are you working tomorrow?"

"Nee. I've got a free day tomorrow."

"Can I come over and see you?"

"Jah! I'd love that." Tara giggled.

"Are you ready, Tara?" William called out.

Tara hugged Megan goodbye. "Come around anytime. I'll be home all day."

CHAPTER 9

Whoever loves instruction loves knowledge, But he who hates correction is stupid.
Proverbs 12:1

TARA GOT INTO BED, reached over to the bedside table, and turned off the lantern. Elizabeth would be the only one who would understand what she was going through right now, since her family had found her recently, but Tara couldn't talk to her because she didn't know exactly where she was. Elizabeth and Joseph were staying at a different family's house every night.

As her head sank into the pillow, her thoughts turned to Mark and the disturbing news she'd heard about Mary Lou. It troubled her more than it normally would've because she was pretty sure she herself had seen the two of them together.

Maybe when Elizabeth got back, she could find out about Mark and Mary Lou, or could get Joseph to find out some things. Sue Anne had most likely gotten things wrong and it was quite possible that they'd only been out together once in his buggy and that was the same time she'd seen them.

TARA WOKE the next morning to the sound of a buggy outside her window. She opened her eyes and it took her a moment to gather where she was. The sunlight streaming in from the window told her she'd slept longer than she'd intended.

She jumped out of bed and looked out the window. It was Mark outside.

What is he doing here at this time of morning?

The last thing she wanted was for him to think he could enter without knocking just because he had a key, so she dressed fast and ran down to the front door.

He had his hand up, apparently about to knock when she opened the door.

"In time for *kaffe,* am I?" he asked with his usual smirk hinting around his lips.

"I suppose I can put some on for you."

He nodded.

"Denke?" She stared at him waiting for a response.

"Oh. Yeah, *denke.*" He looked her up and down. "You're not going to work today?"

"I've got the day off."

He scoffed as he followed her into the kitchen, "You seem to have a lot of those."

"That's because I work part time. You don't seem to be doing much work yourself."

"It's a quiet time of year. I'm starting back at the beginning of February. I saw you in town with Caleb yesterday."

He *had* seen her. "*Jah,* he was good enough to take me to work."

"That was very *nice* of him."

"He's a nice person."

"He's not for you."

She raised her eyebrows and glared at him. He couldn't run away from her and then come back and boss her about as if he owned her. "Says who?"

"Are you going to act like nothing ever happened between us? Is the past going to be swept under the rug?"

"You're the one who chose... chose to leave. I was here all the time. I didn't go anywhere."

"I explained everything to you. I thought you would have some compassion and understanding when I opened my heart and..."

"I'm low on compassion and understanding at the moment. Anyway, I've got far more important things to think about than you running away like a scared rabbit."

"Yeah? Like what?"

"Oh, that's right. You don't know."

"Know what?"

Tara's first instinct was to keep her news from him, but the way news traveled through the community, he'd find out soon anyway. "I met my birth father last night."

"Jah! You told me you were meeting him. How did it go?"

She told him what her father had told her.

"I'm happy for you, Tara. It must make you feel different about yourself."

"It probably should, but it doesn't. It feels good to know that he cares and would've cared back then if he'd known about me. I could've grown up in that family. *My* family. I guess she gave me away because she thought she was going to be a single parent. Things were more difficult back then—Gretchen explained that to me. These days there are more single-parent families than there were back then. Less stigma about it."

"Gott wanted you here in the community that's why. So you could meet me, your husband."

She was certain now that there was nothing between him and Mary Lou.

"I know. That's what William and Gretchen said. Not about marrying, you—the bit about *Gott* wanting me here. They say that all the time, and I guess it's true."

"Now that you know something about your past, how about thinking about your future—with me?"

Her heart was saying yes, but her head was saying no. Before she gave in to her heart again, there were some things she had to know.

"Why didn't you tell me you needed some time alone to think? I would've understood—tried to understand."

He slowly nodded, then said, "I don't know. I guess I didn't want to hurt you."

She leaned forward; she had to be truthful. "You hurt me more by remaining silent and then vanishing."

His gaze lowered. "I needed some space, some time to think. I felt as though I was losing myself in my love for you and trying to become someone I wasn't."

Tara did not understand the nonsense he was carrying on with; it all sounded like gobbledygook to her. "Well, you've got yourself back now and all is well with the world." He looked up at her with raised eyebrows and an open mouth. She continued, "I'm glad you've got that off your chest." She stood up and went to walk away.

He bounded to his feet causing the chair to fall back, and then reached out and grabbed her arm. "Tara wait; I've just told you that I love you."

Tara pulled her arm away. *"Jah*, Mark, I heard, but that's in the past."

"*Nee*, Tara. It doesn't have to be in the past."

"If you will excuse me, Mark, I've got things to do."

"Wait!" She swung around to see him picking up the chair.

"What else is there to say? Finish your *kaffe* and then do whatever it is you have to do around here. I'll be upstairs out of your way."

The corners of his lips turned upward and he laughed.

"What's funny?" she asked.

"Life's so funny."

"There's nothing funny about you leaving me just when we were getting closer. Why would you do that to me, as though I'm some game that you put away when you're bored, and pick up again later when you feel like it?"

His face flushed and his voice rose. "It's not a game. I had to be sure that marriage was right for me, and not just because it's expected for everyone else in the community. What if I wasn't the same as everyone else? I did *not* want to disappoint you. Is that so hard to understand? We were moving too fast."

Tara was silent for a moment while she tried to understand his reasoning. "Why didn't you tell me?"

His face softened and his voice lowered. "Would you have understood?"

She dropped her eyes to the floor and shook her head. "*Nee*, and I don't understand now. What if you suddenly disappear again?"

He took two steps toward her. "That's exactly why I didn't explain my actions to anyone, not even you. No one would have understood. But, I never stopped loving you. It wasn't about love, or about you, it was about me."

She took a step backward.

He swiftly moved in front of her, as close as he could be. "Want to know a secret?"

"Aha," she said softly as she looked up into his dark eyes.

"Joseph never asked me to do anything here. I heard you were staying in the *haus* and I took the opportunity to be alone with you to explain myself. Joseph gave me a spare key for emergencies."

Tara opened her mouth in shock at his audacity. He took his chance and swiftly lowered his mouth to kiss her. She ducked out of his way.

He drew his head back and took both her hands in his. "Say you'll marry me, but for real this time?"

She shook her head. *"Nee."* Seeing his tools by the door, she said, "Don't forget to take all your tools with you." She walked to the front door and held it open.

"I won't give up," he said as he walked over to his wooden tool box, grabbed it, and then walked out the door.

She closed the door and leaned against it. When she gave her heart, it would be to someone who she'd feel safe with. He didn't have to be the most desirable man in the community, or the best looking, as long as he was a man she could trust.

Closing her eyes, she heard Mark's buggy horse clip-clop away from the house. When relief washed over her like a warm shower on a cold night, she knew she'd done the right thing.

She shook her head, trying to shake away all remnants of the man she'd once thought so highly of.

CHAPTER 10

Charm is deceitful and beauty is passing,
But a woman who fears the Lord,
she shall be praised.
Proverbs 31:30

WHEN REDMOND ARRIVED BACK HOME after visiting Tara, he paid the babysitter and then got Brandon on the phone and asked him to come to the house. Redmond was anxious to relieve himself of his wife's long-held secret.

"What's this about, Dad?" Brandon said as he came through the front door.

"It's something very important." Redmond sat his son and daughter down in the living room and started right from the beginning, starting at the tumultuous relationship that he'd had with Avalon's mother. And then he went on to explain that they'd separated for over a year and then gotten back together. Brandon had been a toddler at the time of their separation.

Brandon and Avalon sat in silence as they listened to the whole story.

"We have a sister?" Avalon asked, her eyes bulging.

Redmond nodded.

"I can't believe Mom kept that from us," Brandon said about the only woman he remembered as his mother.

"She thought it best. Tara had been adopted before we reunited, and she wouldn't have wanted to disrupt her life."

"And you've met her?"

"Yes. I've just come back from meeting her at her foster family's house."

"Does she know about us?"

"She does now, and she wants to meet you if you want to meet her."

"Of course we do," Brandon said while Avalon nodded enthusiastically.

"What do you think about it, Avalon?"

"Weird. Why didn't you and Mom try to get her back?"

"Dad already said he didn't know anything about her. Weren't you listening?" Brandon said.

"Yeah, well, Mom should've done something. What if that had happened to you or me?"

"It did. She's one of us. Just the same."

"When can we meet her?" Avalon asked her father.

"She'll call me soon."

"Call her and tell her we want to meet her as soon as possible," Brandon suggested.

"She doesn't have a cell phone. She's been raised Amish for the past few years."

"Oh, man!" Brandon hit his head. "Are you serious?"

"No electricity, no Playstation, and all that? No car?" Avalon asked.

Redmond nodded. "I met the foster family and they're very nice people. Tara had been adopted twice and both times it didn't work out."

"Why?" Brandon asked.

"I don't know really. I suppose she'll share more when she feels more comfortable."

"Does she look like me?" Avalon asked.

"There's a resemblance. She looks a lot like my mother did as a girl."

Brandon frowned. "So, we just wait for her to call you?"

Redmond nodded. "If she hasn't called in a week or so, I can always pay her another visit."

"What was the family like?"

"Very quiet, and humble, softly spoken."

"What about their house?" Avalon asked.

"Smallish, neat and clean. They had gas overhead lighting, so it was a little dark."

"Are you sure it was dark, or maybe you just didn't have your glasses on," Brandon joked.

"Yeah, Dad. You're supposed to wear your glasses all the time."

He scratched the bridge of his nose. "I think if I wear them too much my eyes will become dependant on them."

"You're vain, that's what it is," Brandon said with a laugh.

"Yeah," Avalon agreed.

Ignoring their teasing, Redmond continued, "I thought we should have Tara join us for dinner one night and I want you both to be on your best behavior. Keep in mind that she might be a little standoffish and shy."

"Yeah, we're not stupid, Dad. We'll try not to scare her away."

"Brandon would scare her away," Avalon said.

Brandon picked up a cushion and hit his sister with it. Then she did the same to him.

"Stop it! And don't do things like that while she's here, whatever you do."

"We won't." Avalon giggled.

"Now I've got another sister to boss me about," Brandon said.

Redmond was pleased that his children had taken the news well. If only his wife were still alive.

CHAPTER 11

To every thing there is a season, and a time to every purpose
under the heaven: A time to be born, and a time to die; a
time to plant,
and a time to pluck up that which is planted;
Ecclesiastes 3:1

TARA WAS WASHING up her breakfast dishes when she saw William's buggy heading toward the house. It had to be Megan driving it. Looking forward to having someone to talk to, she came to the quick conclusion that living alone wasn't for her.

She dried her hands on a tea towel and went to open the door. As soon as Megan had tied up the horse, she hurried over to Tara.

"I came as soon as I could. Let's go out somewhere. I haven't been out for a long time."

"I'm glad to hear that you want to go out. We can go to a coffee shop in town. I've got lots to tell you," Tara said.

"Lots? Since last night?"

Tara nodded.

"Okay let's go now. We'll go to the one where Elizabeth works."

"Do you want to have a look around the house first?" Tara asked.

"Nee. I've seen it before with Elizabeth before the wedding. Let's just go."

"Sounds good to me. I've just eaten, though, but I could do with another cup of coffee."

Tara grabbed her coat, found her key and was careful to lock the door, wishing that Joseph had never given Mark a key.

As they traveled down the winding roads, Megan asked, "What is it you want to tell me?"

"I'm going to call Redmond today and tell him that I want to meet my sister and my brother."

"That's good. I'm sure they'll be happy to meet you."

"I hope so."

"What else? You look like you've got something else on your mind."

"Do I?" Tara breathed out heavily. "Mark was here this morning."

"Did you ask him about Mary Lou?"

"*Nee*, I didn't. He said he wants to marry me, so I don't think it's true about Mary Lou."

Megan gasped. "What did you say?"

"I said, 'No.' I can't marry him if I can't trust him."

"You should've asked him about Mary Lou."

"I don't know. Anyway, it doesn't matter."

"Do you still love him?"

Tara swallowed hard. She couldn't help the feelings in her heart. "I guess I do."

"Why didn't you say you'd marry him? You're not making sense."

"I am so. He vanished and no one knew where he was, or if they did, no one told me. We were talking about marriage before he disappeared. And now he comes back and when he feels ready, he expects me to be ready."

"What does that matter? It sounds to me like you want the upper hand."

"He hurt me. I don't want to feel like that anymore. I get a hollow feeling in my stomach. Mark says it's because I was adopted that I fear being left alone and that's why I was upset that he went away so suddenly."

"Maybe."

"Well, then that's his excuse for doing anything he wants. I just can't see that I should be okay with him hurting me like that. He would've known I'd be upset about it and he didn't care enough about me. He cared more about himself."

"You want someone who'll put you first?"

Tara nodded. *"Jah,* exactly. That's how it's supposed to be."

"That's how it's supposed to be, but everyone's human, don't forget. People make mistakes and we're supposed to forgive them."

"Yeah, I can forgive him. That doesn't mean I have to marry him."

Megan giggled. "That's true."

"Anyway, since when are you Mark's biggest fan?"

Megan whipped her eyes away from the road to glance at her. "I'm not. I told you what I heard about him. I believe what Sue Anne said. You're the one who said you loved him."

"Yeah, well I'm working on talking myself out of that."

Megan giggled again. "You're so strong, Tara. I don't think I could ever be as strong as you."

"I don't think you'll ever have to be. You'll be just like Elizabeth, and everything will fall into place for you. The perfect man will come along at the perfect time and you'll be the most perfect *fraa."*

"You think so?"

"Yeah."

MEGAN AND TARA sat down at a table in the back of the coffee shop. There was one menu on the table. Tara passed it to Megan.

"See what you want."

"I'm not hungry," Megan said pushing the menu back to Tara.

"Me either. I think I'll just have a coffee."

"Me too."

A waiter came up to their table. Tara recognized him from when she had met Elizabeth there before the wedding. She placed her hand on her bag, which she'd placed where she always did, on the side of the table. "Just a coffee for me."

"Black?" he asked.

"Yes, thanks."

"I'll have a white coffee thanks," Megan said, smiling up at him.

"Nothing to eat?" he said. Tara noticed he didn't return the smile.

"No."

He grabbed the menu and walked away.

"He's a weird one," Tara said before she could stop herself.

"Do you know him?"

Tara shook her head. "No. Don't worry."

"Are you working tomorrow?"

"*Jah,* until three."

"Have you forgotten about Connie and Devon's wedding?"

"I did. I would've completely forgotten if you hadn't mentioned it. I don't finish work until three. I could go after that. I'll have to miss most of it."

"I can come and get you from work when you finish."

"Would you?"

"Of course."

"Denke."

"No one ever thought Connie would marry. Just as well Devon came along when he did."

"Jah. He came to his aunt's funeral didn't he?" Tara asked.

"That's right. Then they fell in love before they got back to his *onkel's haus."*

Tara stuck her nose in the air. "See? It's easy for some."

Megan giggled.

"Megan, why don't you come with me when I meet my sister and brother?"

The waiter brought their coffees to the table. Tara grabbed her bag and put it in her lap. After he'd placed their drinks on the table, he walked away.

"Well?" Tara asked as she perched her bag back on the edge of the table.

"Nee, I couldn't. I'm no good at meeting new people. I wouldn't know what to say."

"Just be there next to me. You don't have to say a thing if you don't want to."

Megan pulled a face. "I will if you want me to."

"Really?"

Megan nodded. "Okay."

"Denke. I feel a lot better now."

"You were nervous?"

"Jah. You're not the only one who gets scared."

"I'm shy. I'm not scared." Megan ripped open a packet of sugar and poured it into her coffee.

"You don't have to be shy."

"That's just the way I've always been. You've never been that way; you wouldn't understand. You've always been good with people. That's why you work in a store and talk to strangers every day."

Tara took a sip of her hot coffee. "Other people are just like you and me."

"When are you meeting your family?"

"Sometime soon. Maybe next week, I guess. I'm calling Redmond later today."

"Let me know and I'll be ready."

When they heard a loud knock on the window of the café, they turned to see the Tomkin brothers who were waving at them as they walked past. Tara and Megan smiled and waved back at them.

"Do you like one of them? They're handsome and they're our age," Tara asked.

"Nee. I'm hoping there might be someone new at Connie's wedding."

Suddenly Megan grabbed Tara's hand. "Look over there, across the road, Tara."

Tara looked through the large window of the coffee shop to see Mary Lou and Mark walking together. Close together.

"That must've been her I saw in his buggy the other day. I thought it was, but I wasn't all that certain."

"See? I told you he's been seeing a lot of her."

Tara nodded. "Why did he ask me to marry him when he's spending time with her?"

They stared at him.

"They both seem to be enjoying each other's company," Megan said.

"Yeah, a little too much if you ask me. I think Sue Anne was right."

"I told you."

"Yeah, yeah."

"Don't worry, Tara, Elizabeth told me that Caleb likes you."

"Caleb?" Tara acted like Elizabeth had never mentioned him to her.

"Jah. Caleb, Joseph's *bruder."*

"I know who he is. He drove me to work and back the other day."

"And to the *haus* the other day," Megan reminded her.

"Oh, yeah. I forgot about that."

Megan lowered her head keeping her eyes fixed onto Tara. "Is there anything you'd like to share with me, Tara?"

Tara giggled. "Just that he's talking a little more."

"Ah, so that's why you refused Mark's proposal."

She looked out the window, and the couple they'd been studying had moved on.

"Nee, Megan. I don't think so."

"Hmmm."

Tara giggled. "You sound just like Aunt Gretchen."

"That's where I learned to say 'hmmm.'"

"And you've got the same look on your face as she gets when she's suspicious about something, or she doesn't believe us."

Megan laughed and then wagged her finger just like William often did. "I'll be keeping an eye on you and Caleb at the wedding tomorrow."

The two of them laughed.

MEGAN COLLECTED Tara from work at three o'clock. The ceremony had taken place at one o'clock, but people would still be socializing and eating. And those two things were Tara's favorite pastimes.

"How was the wedding?" Tara asked.

"Really good."

Tara wanted to learn about Mark and find out if he was hanging around close to Mary Lou, but she didn't like to ask.

"Was anybody interesting there—anybody new?" Tara asked knowing that Megan had been hoping that there would be.

"I saw two men who looked nice. One of them smiled at me. I think they were brothers; they looked similar."

"Point them out to me when we get there."

"Nee. Not if you're going to do something embarrassing."

"Embarrassing like what?"

"Like being obvious and dragging me over to introduce me to them."

"Well, how are you going to meet them if I don't do that?"

Megan rolled her eyes. "Just forget it."

"I mean it. Tell me, how are you going to do that?"

"Do what?" Megan asked.

Tara's head was elsewhere; she was trying to talk with Megan and thinking about Mark, and also Caleb, all at the same time.

"What I meant to say is, how are you going to talk to them if you don't make an effort?"

"They can come and talk to me."

Tara stared at Megan, blinking rapidly. "They haven't yet, have they?"

"Nee, so that means they can't be interested."

"They might be ridiculously shy like you."

Megan's mouth fell open. "I am not."

"You are so."

"I am not."

"I'm already making my plans to go over and talk to them," Tara said.

"If you go over and talk to them, I'll go and tell Mark that you're going to marry him."

Tara laughed. "It's hardly the same thing."

Megan giggled. "Well, just don't you dare do it."

CHAPTER 12

*Be careful for nothing; but in every thing by prayer and
supplication with thanksgiving let your requests be made
known unto God.*
Philippians 4:6

WHEN THEY PULLED into the driveway of Connie's
parents' house where the wedding was held, they had
to park their buggy a long way away due to the seem-
ingly hundreds of buggies that were there.

"This is a popular wedding,"

"I think there are a lot of relatives on both sides."

"It seems like it," Megan said.

"Now show me where those boys are," Tara said.

"Nee, Tara. Don't be embarrassing."

"I won't say anything if you really don't want me to, you have my word on it. Just point them out to me."

"Are you certain you won't embarrass me?"

"Not over that. But I might embarrass you over something else."

"Good."

"But first I need food. I'm starving. I didn't eat lunch just so I could make more room."

Megan secured the horse and the two girls walked quickly into Connie's house.

Tara couldn't help looking around for Mark and Caleb. She was a little disappointed that Caleb hadn't visited to find out what happened when she met her father.

After taking a plate, Tara helped herself to food from one of the many tables that ran down the length of the house.

Glancing at Megan standing beside her, she asked, "Have you already eaten?"

"Jah. I couldn't fit another thing in if I tried. Except until the dessert comes out, and I'm hoping that's soon."

Tara giggled and then her attention turned to filling her plate with more of her favorite foods.

"Where are we sitting?" Tara asked when she couldn't fit any more on her plate.

"Follow me."

They sat down where they had a good view of two

handsome young men Tara had never met before. She leaned over to Megan, and whispered, "Is that them?"

"Please be quiet; they'll hear you."

"*Nee,* they won't."

Megan rolled her eyes.

"I agree with you. I mean, what you said about them before."

Megan smiled.

Tara could see the boys glancing in Megan's direction. She hoped it wouldn't be long before one of them came over to say hello. That was the only hope Megan had, because there was no way Megan would get to talk with them if they didn't make the move.

When Tara was halfway through her food, someone sat down next to her. She turned to see that it was Caleb.

"Hello, Tara."

"Hello."

"Have you just finished work?"

Tara nodded.

"I came to visit you yesterday, but there was no one home. "

"Did you? Oh, I must've been out with Megan. We went into town. What did you come to see me about?"

He smiled. "To see how things went with your father?"

"Really good. He explained everything to me, and I have a sister and a half brother."

"A half brother and a sister?"

"Jah, it's a long story."

"I've got a lot of time."

Tara was pleased he was interested. She told him all that Redmond O'Donnell had told her.

"That's an interesting story."

"I know. And he would've wanted me if he'd known about me."

"It's good that you know your past and how you came to be adopted. It puts an end to you not knowing and having to wonder."

"I feel different inside. I don't know why. I guess it shouldn't make any difference. But it's answered all the questions that I've had. Well, not all of the questions. I've still got a million questions I want to ask him."

"Can I take you home when the wedding's over, Tara?"

Tara smiled. "I'd like that."

A smile brightened his face. "Good. I see someone I need to say hello to. I'll meet up with you a bit later."

"Okay."

When he was gone, Tara turned around to look for Megan, expecting her to have gone to visit with some of the other guests. "Oh. Were you sitting there all that time?"

"What was I supposed to do?"

"I'm sorry, I was too caught up with Caleb to think that I had my back to you."

"It's okay. You were obviously focused on Caleb."

"He's driving me home."

"I know. I heard."

"Well, what do you think about him?"

"I like him. You're relaxed with him."

"I like him too. I used to think he was a bit strange because he was so quiet."

"Same as me?"

Tara pulled a face. "Yeah well, you can't get to know someone when they don't talk. It's like they think that I don't like them or something."

"What are you talking about?"

"I thought Caleb didn't like me because he never talked when he was around me. And now that we're seeing more of each other, he's starting to talk more. That's why you should stop being so quiet; no one can get to know you."

"It's just hard for me. I'm not as confident as you."

"Just try. Come over with me now and we'll talk to those two." She nodded toward the two men Megan had been talking about.

Megan giggled. "We can't do that."

Tara noticed that Megan's gaze had locked onto something.

"What is it?"

"It's Mark and he's walking this way. I'll leave you two alone to talk."

"*Nee.* Don't leave me." It was too late. Megan was already out of her chair and Mark was getting ready to sit on it.

SAMANTHA PRICE

"I was wondering where you were. I was nearly going to go to the house to find you."

"I was working."

"I'm sorry how things were between us the other day. I don't want us to fight. You know how I want things to be."

"I know how you *tell* me you want things to be, but I should let you know that there are rumors about you and Mary Lou."

When he gulped noticeably, she knew that it must've been true. She stared at him, waiting for an answer. When none came, she continued, "I saw you in town with her the other day and I've heard a lot of talk since then, so I guess it's true."

"She's just a friend."

"That's what we used to tell people. Or, more accurately, that's what you told me to tell everyone."

"Nee. She *is* just a friend."

"I think she's more than that. What were you going to do if I'd said yes? How do you think Mary Lou would feel about that?"

"It's not like that. We're just friends. I keep telling you that. Why are you giving me such a hard time?" He hunched his shoulders and pulled the neck of his coat up.

"I know you well enough to know that what you're telling me is not quite right."

He was lying, but she didn't like to flat out accuse him of lying.

"Don't you want to get married, Tara?"

"Jah, I do, but I will only marry someone I can trust."

He leaned forward and traced his finger along her hand as it rested on the table. She pulled her hand away from him and placed it in her lap.

"You're being silly, Tara. You can trust me."

"Time will tell."

"What does that mean?"

"Exactly what I said."

"So, you're going to make me wait, and then what?"

"Mark, I'm not doing anything to you. I'm certainly not making you wait for me or anything else."

"What if I asked Mary Lou to marry me—would you be jealous?"

She stared into his eyes. She'd be upset if he married someone else. He wouldn't, would he?

"I've got too much going on at the moment."

He leaned in and whispered, "I'm not going to wait around for you because you might still reject me and then I would've missed my chance with Mary Lou." He stood up and walked away.

It was true! She stared at the nearly empty plate in front of her and stopped herself from picking it up and throwing at the back of his head.

"They're bringing the desserts out now, Tara."

She looked up to see Megan. "Good. Just in time."

CHAPTER 13

*But that no man is justified by the law in the sight of God, it
is evident: for, The just shall live by faith.*
Galatians 3:11

TARA WAS PLEASED when the wedding was over so she
could escape and be with Caleb. Looking around for
him, she saw Mark and Mary Lou standing close to
each other, talking with barely an inch between them.
She was upset to see them together, but more than that,
she was upset about the way Mark had treated her. She
was glad she hadn't gotten sucked into his flattery.

"Are you ready?"

She turned around and looked into Caleb's pleasant
face.

"Yeah, I'm ready. I'll just say goodbye to Megan."

After she said goodbye to her and a few more people, she hurried to the buggy with Caleb without bothering to look over at Mark. Caleb and Tara walked past the bishop and his wife and they exchanged nods. Tara had never had much to do with them.

Mark wasn't interested in her as an individual it seemed, he just wanted to get married to somebody. Now, that somebody was most likely Mary Lou.

"It seems to be getting colder," Caleb said as soon as they were both in the buggy.

Tara pulled her shawl tighter around her. "Certainly does."

"I've been thinking about getting one of those heaters to put in the buggy, but I don't drive it enough to make it worthwhile."

"It's okay. It's not that far to Elizabeth's house."

As they drove down the winding roads, Tara was pleased that she'd gotten to know Caleb. Maybe he was the man God had intended for her to be with. A loud crash coming from nowhere coincided with the buggy coming to a halt.

"What's wrong?" Tara looked over at Caleb who looked worried.

"I don't know. I'll get out and take a look."

Caleb jumped out of the buggy and Tara leaped out after him. She joined him as he was looking at the rear wheel.

He looked up at her. "Tara, get back in the buggy. It's too cold out here."

"Is the wheel broken?"

"Nee, it's not broken. I can fix it."

"Well, what's happened to it?"

"Tara, get back in the buggy!"

She looked at him, surprised that he could be so forceful. He took her by the arm and marched her back into the buggy. Then he pulled a blanket out of the back and covered her with it.

Wagging, his finger at her, he said, "Sit there until I fix it."

She gave no response and neither did he wait for one. He strode back to attend to the wheel. Tara pulled the blanket around her shoulders. She felt safe and protected around Caleb. He was turning out to be a real man.

The next thing she knew he was by the side of the road dragging a fence post that had fallen over, pulling it back toward the buggy. Then he appeared beside her.

"I might need you out of the buggy for one moment. I need the buggy as light as possible."

She got out of the buggy and the freezing air bit into her cheeks.

He rubbed her on the back. "Are you okay?"

Shivering, she nodded. He pulled off his coat and placed it gently around her shoulders even though she still had the blanket on.

"You'll need your coat, or you'll freeze."

"Nee. I'm getting too hot," he said heading back to the rear of the buggy.

SAMANTHA PRICE

With the help of the large post, the buggy tipped over to one side while he tended to the wheel.

"Okay, Tara, you can get back in now."

As she climbed back into the buggy, she saw him discard the old fence post.

She wanted to get out and see if she could help, but she knew he would only tell her off again, so she waited patiently, which wasn't easy for her.

He retrieved the toolbox from the back of the buggy and several minutes later, after some hammering, they were ready to go.

"Are you okay?"

She could see that the concern on his face was real. He was more attentive and caring than Mark had ever been.

She nodded. "I'm fine. What about you?"

"I'm okay. Sorry about that."

"You couldn't help it."

"Well, it's ruined our buggy ride."

It was then that she realized that he was looking on this as a date, and not merely driving her home for convenience sake. She wondered what the bishop had thought about her going in a buggy with Caleb.

Now looking at the snow-covered view, she said, "I don't recognize this road."

He glanced over at her and smiled. "I'm taking you on a nicer drive home."

She giggled. "That explains it. I don't know all these back roads."

When they neared the house, Tara was amazed to see that Mark's buggy was there.

"That's Mark!" Caleb said.

"Why's he here? I was only just talking to him at the wedding and he mentioned nothing of coming here."

"Strange."

Once they pulled up, they both got out to meet Mark. He was on the porch leaning against the front door with his arms folded.

As they approached, he stepped forward. "Where have the two of you been?"

"I just drove her home from the wedding," Caleb said.

"Why are you even here, Caleb?"

"Don't be rude, Mark. He was kind enough to drive me home."

"Where have you two been?" he asked again.

"We had a bit of trouble with the buggy and that's why it took us some time to get here."

He dipped his head and his dark eyes were looking straight at Caleb. "I came straight here from the wedding and I didn't pass you."

"Well…" Tara started to explain and was cut off by Mark.

"What's going on here, Caleb? Tara and I are in a relationship and you're coming in between us."

Tara gasped at his lie. A few weeks ago it would've been true, but he as good as said if she wouldn't marry him he'd ask Mary Lou.

"I'm sorry, I didn't realize," Caleb said softly taking a step back.

"You don't have to go, Caleb."

Caleb turned around. "I'll talk to you later, Tara."

When he kept walking, Tara glared at Mark. "Are you happy now?"

"What do you think you were doing just now?"

"What are you doing with Mary Lou?"

"I told you we're just friends."

"You said if I didn't marry you...." she looked around at Caleb to see him leaving. "Now that Caleb is gone, you had better go too."

"Why? Worried about your reputation?"

"My reputation is fine. Now please leave."

He stood still with his hands on his hips for a few moments before he walked over to his buggy. He turned to face her. "I don't know what you're playing at."

"Goodbye, Mark." She walked inside and slammed the door behind her. She waited until she heard his buggy leave and then she collapsed onto the couch.

She felt awful that Caleb would think there was something still going on between her and Mark. If she'd only spoken up and said there was nothing going on, but surely Caleb knew that.

Why did Caleb take her the long way home? It had to be because he liked her and wanted to spend more time with her. Now she had to convince Caleb that Mark and she were over for good.

CHAPTER 14

But seek ye first the kingdom of God, and his righteousness;
and all these things shall be added unto you.
Matthew 6:33

WHEN TARA WALKED outside the quilting store for her lunch break, Megan was right outside waiting for her.

"What are you doing here?" Tara asked.

"Waiting for you."

"Why didn't you come inside? It's freezing out here."

"I didn't want you to get into trouble. You know how Mrs. Thomas complained about you having so many friends calling in to see you."

"Jah, that's true. Come to the coffee shop with me."

They linked arms and walked up the street.

"I came here to tell you that the bishop wants to see you this afternoon."

"Wants to see me?"

"Jah."

"Why?"

"I don't know. Did you do something?"

"Not that I'm aware of."

"William and Gretchen arranged for me to drive you there when you finish work. Did you get a taxi this morning?"

Tara nodded, disturbed by the bishop wanting to see her. It had to be because she'd unknowingly done something bad.

"What does he want to see me about?"

"He didn't say."

"Well, what do Gretchen and William think it's about?"

"They don't know either. I guess you'll just have to wait and see."

"I hope I haven't done anything wrong."

Megan laughed. "Wouldn't you know if you had?"

Tara pulled a face. "I guess so. I don't think I have."

"He's probably just asking if you want to stay on in the community, or if you're going to get baptized, things like that."

"He didn't ask Elizabeth any of those things and she's younger than both of us. Has he asked you?"

Megan shook her head.

They sat and had something to eat in the coffee

shop while Tara told Megan what had happened when she arrived home the night before.

"Mark must've seen you go home with Caleb and it made him really jealous."

"It seems like it. It makes me wonder about a few things."

"And how do you feel about Caleb?"

"I like him; he seems really nice. I don't think he's had a girlfriend before. Do you know if he has?"

"I wouldn't know if he has or hasn't. You're asking the wrong person."

Tara took a bite of her bacon pie. There had been no sign of Caleb this morning and she had hoped that he would come by to drive her to work.

"Have you called your father yet to arrange that meeting?"

"No. I'll do that before I go back to work. I hope his children want to meet me."

"They will. Don't worry."

"I hope you're right."

SEVERAL MINUTES later when they'd finished eating, Tara had Megan stand next to her while she called Redmond, her birth father. They arranged to meet for dinner next week. Tara hung up the phone.

"He said he'll pick us up from Grabers' house on Tuesday evening."

"Okay, that sounds good. So, that means they all want to meet you?"

"Yeah, he said so."

"That's great. I knew they would."

Tara nodded, glad that Megan had so much confidence about her siblings wanting to meet her.

"I better let you get back to work. How are you getting home?"

"It's okay. I'll get a taxi. I'll just have a look around the shops first before I go home."

"Are you sure?"

"Yes. Oh, wait. Didn't I have to go to the bishop's this afternoon?"

Megan hit her head. "That's right."

Both girls laughed at their forgetfulness.

WHEN THE GIRLS arrived at the bishop's house, the bishop's wife had Megan wait in a sitting room while Tara was taken into another room. There were two couches in the room and Tara sat down on the one opposite Bishop John. The bishop's wife, Ruth, sat next to him.

"How about some hot tea, Ruth?" the bishop asked.

"The pot is boiling," she answered.

The Bishop nodded and then looked at Tara. "It's a rather delicate subject I'd like to discuss with you, Tara."

"Have I done something wrong?"

"*Nee*, but some things have come to my attention

and there has been talk. I wanted to caution you to be aware."

"I'll just go and check on that tea," the Bishop's wife said before she headed out of the room.

"Be aware of what?"

"Perhaps I'll wait until Ruth comes back into the room. She's good at helping me explain things."

Tara nodded.

"William tells me you're working at a quilting store in town?"

"I work there a few days a week. It's only a part-time job, but I really enjoy it."

The bishop nodded. "That's good. And Gretchen tells me that your father has contacted you recently?"

"That's right." Tara glanced at the bishop's large Bible that was next to him on the couch. She wondered if he was going to preach out of it to her. If she hadn't done anything wrong, it certainly made her feel like she had.

The bishop's wife came back in with a tray of tea, cookies and cake.

"This looks lovely," Tara said, feeling slightly hungry.

"It's an apple cake. It's my mother's recipe. My family had an orchard and that's probably why I always cook with so many apples. It's a habit really."

"Tara is *not* here to speak about apples, Ruth!"

Ruth stopped pouring the tea and handed a cup to Tara. "*Jah,* I'm sorry, Tara. Once I get started talking about apples, sometimes I just can't stop. It's because I grew up amongst them and have a fondness for them."

"That's alright. I like hearing what people did when they were growing up. I'm going to meet my family soon. I've met my father, and soon I'll meet my sister and my half-brother."

"William told us that your father came to the house."

"Yes. It was quite a surprise when he made contact. Especially after Elizabeth was just found by her family."

Ruth offered her a cookie and she took one while balancing the tea cup and saucer on her knees. Her eyes were drawn to the cake, but since no one else had taken a piece, she didn't want to be the first to do so. She politely sipped her tea, avoiding looking at the cake that was silently calling to her.

"Ruth, I was waiting for you to get back before I continued telling Tara why I wanted her here."

Ruth nodded. "Go ahead."

"Tara, I just want you to be aware that, just because some men belong to the community, it does not mean that they are completely trustworthy and will not take advantage if you let them."

Tara's eyes grew wide. Was he talking about one person in particular? *"Denke* for the warning."

"Have you heard about a wolf in sheep's clothing?"

"I think so. That means someone in disguise, I'd say."

"Jah. There might be some men who are thinking of

leaving our community and are not totally abiding by the *Ordnung.*"

"I see. That's a good point. I'd never thought of things like that."

"You should," Ruth blurted out.

"Are you talking about one man in particular?"

"It would be wrong of me to call someone by name. But I can say this to you, sometimes it's the quietest of men that you have to watch out for."

"I understand, but can't you give me a hint?"

The bishop glanced at his wife and then his bushy eyebrows drew together as he looked back at Tara. "This person might have an interest in leaving us and working on cars. Now, that's all I can say in my position."

"You must be strong to stay on the narrow path, Tara," Ruth said. "Wide is the road that leads to destruction and narrow's the way."

"Got it. Narrow path." Tara nodded recalling the subject of the bishop's favorite sermon.

"I hope you'll stay with us after you meet your *familye,* as Elizabeth did," Ruth said.

The bishop turned to his wife. "Now that I've said what I have to say, you can invite Megan to have tea with us."

Ruth sprang to her feet and obeyed her husband.

Megan walked into the room with Ruth and sat down beside Tara. They had a lovely talk with the bishop and to Tara's surprise, Megan was bold enough to take the first piece of cake. Tara happily followed her lead.

ON THE WAY home from the bishop's house, Tara told Megan everything that the bishop and his wife had said to her.

"He was giving you a warning."

"Obviously. I was right not to have anything to do with Mark when he came back. I should never have trusted him—ever."

"Mark?"

"*Jah.* Don't you think the bishop was talking about Mark?" Tara asked.

"*Nee.* I don't. Didn't he say a sheep in wolf's clothing?"

Tara giggled. "It was the other way 'round. Wait a minute… a wolf in sheep's clothing. That's right." She looked over at Megan to see she wasn't laughing. "What do you mean and why are you looking so worried?"

"Well, doesn't that describe Caleb?"

Tara gasped. "*Jah.* And the bishop did talk about someone appearing quiet. He said it's the quiet ones I have to watch."

"I thought right away, as soon as you told me what he'd said, that he was talking about Caleb."

Tara's tummy squirmed. "And at the wedding, the bishop saw me leaving with Caleb, so that fits too."

"He must know things about Caleb that we don't know."

"I've got a bad history with men already and I'm not even nineteen years old."

"Things could've been worse. If the bishop hadn't warned you, who knows what might have happened?"

Tara put a hand over her tummy. "And I was really starting to like him."

"He seemed nice. What if he'd tried to attack a woman and she fought back and that's how he got those scars?"

"Nee. Elizabeth said he's had them for a long time. But, you know what else?"

"What?"

"When he took me home last night, he went the long way and then something happened to the buggy wheel. We were alone for some time in the middle of nowhere."

"Did he try anything?"

"Nee, but he might have intended to and then changed his mind. When we got back to the *haus,* Mark was there."

"Mark has probably heard about Caleb and was trying to protect you."

"That doesn't excuse him for being too friendly with Mary Lou."

"What did he say when you asked about Mary Lou?"

Tara shook her head. "He told me at the wedding if

I didn't marry him, he'd marry Mary Lou. Other times he insists that they're just friends."

"When you're not ready to announce a relationship, you have to say you're just friends. I don't know, Tara. It seems you can't trust either of them."

Tara nodded. "I feel like such a fool for starting to like Caleb. He just seemed so trustworthy."

CHAPTER 15

While the earth remaineth, seedtime and harvest, and cold and heat, and summer and winter, and day and night shall not cease.
Genesis 8:22

TARA WAS glad that both Caleb and Mark kept away from her for the next few days. She had time to think about meeting her siblings.

On Tuesday afternoon, Tara took a taxi from work straight to William and Gretchen's house to wait for Redmond to collect her and Megan.

Tara sat in the kitchen watching Megan help Gretchen with making dinner.

"Just be yourself. They'll be more worried about whether you like them," Aunt Gretchen said.

"I think I'm more scared than she is," Megan said with a giggle.

"You just have to be yourself too, Megan. Stop concentrating on how you feel and start thinking how the other people feel. Don't be nervous. Concentrate on putting them at ease."

"Thanks for the advice, *Mamm.* I will," Megan said.

"I AM SO glad you called me, Tara," Redmond said.

"Didn't you think I was going to?"

"I was a little concerned that you might not. Your brother and sister are looking forward to meeting you. Avalon can't stop asking questions about you. Brandon just takes things as they come."

"How did they take the news when you told them about me?"

"They were shocked naturally, but they're very eager to meet you."

"Good. I'm looking forward to meeting them too."

"If you don't mind me asking, how did it come about that you were adopted twice? The social worker didn't tell me too much."

"I don't mind you asking at all. The first time—I don't remember much, but I learned later that the wife died. I probably was with them since I was born virtually until I was about eight—"

"I heard it was younger," Megan said.

"It could've been. Gretchen knows it all. When I

was adopted with the first people, the wife died and I was relinquished. I think that's the term used. Then I was adopted again, but I wasn't well behaved. I don't know why. I had a lot of anger, I guess, and I just didn't want to do anything I was told."

"And how long have you been with the Grabers? I'm sure you told me the other night, but there was a lot to take in."

"I've been with the Grabers for a few years."

"I'm sorry things worked out the way they did."

"There's no need to be sorry; things work out how they were supposed to work out."

"Well, I wish it had been supposed to work out differently."

"We've met now, so that's a good thing."

"It is."

THEY EVENTUALLY PULLED up at Redmond's house.

"Is this where you live?"

"It is."

"It's very big."

"Yes, Marjorie liked spacious houses. Now, Brandon and Avalon have been in charge of the dinner, so I hope it works out well. Brandon tells me he's a pretty good cook. He's lived away from home for two years, and he enjoys cooking."

"Oh, he's here tonight just to see me?"

"He is."

Redmond parked in the driveway and then they walked to the front door.

When Redmond opened the door, Brandon and Avalon were there to meet her. Brandon was as tall as Redmond, handsome, with light brown hair and a wide smile. Avalon was tall for her age, with the same dark hair as Tara, and she wore jeans and a T-shirt.

Redmond introduced everybody. Then Avalon started talking at a mile a minute and Tara had to smile. Avalon's personality was similar to her own. Redmond walked everybody through to the living room and they sat down for a while.

Tara took a minute to glance over at Megan to make sure she wasn't feeling too awkward. Megan was looking relaxed, engrossed in a conversation with Brandon.

Avalon got right down to asking all the nitty-gritty questions.

When Tara was in the middle of answering one of her questions, Avalon suddenly jumped to her feet. "I found something; I'll just go get it and show you."

She ran out of the room and came back a moment later holding a photograph. She placed it in Tara's hands.

"I think this is you," Avalon said.

Tara stared at the small photo of a woman with a newborn in her arms. The woman was smiling and looked proud, so it had to be her baby. She looked up at Redmond. "Is this me and my mother?"

"It could well be. It's Marjorie for certain. I haven't seen that photo before. The baby's not Brandon or Avalon," Redmond said.

"I found it in Mom's box one day. I asked her who it was. I expected her to say Brandon, or me, but she slapped my hand and told me I had no right going through her things. She acted really strange and now I know why."

Tara stared back at the photo. If her mother had kept a photo of her all those years, surely that meant that she cared about her.

"Can I keep this?" Tara asked.

"Yes. Would you like to see more photos of Mom and us?"

"I sure would."

"How about we leave that until after dinner?" Redmond looked over at Brandon who was conversing with Megan.

"Brandon, how's the dinner coming along?"

"Should we have it now? It's all ready to go."

Redmond nodded. "We might as well have it now."

Brandon headed out of the room. A moment later, he yelled for Avalon to help him.

Megan jumped to her feet and said to Avalon, "I can help him if you want to stay talking with Tara."

"You're a guest."

"You'd be doing Megan a favor; she loves being in the kitchen," Tara said.

Avalon giggled. "I don't."

Megan hurried to the kitchen and Tara was pleased that Megan was finally coming out of her shell. It was a big step for her to offer to help in the kitchen and especially to be alone with a man. With Brandon, Megan didn't seem awkward or shy at all.

"Dinner smells amazing. What is it?" Tara asked.

"It's roast lamb and vegetables. Brandon wanted to do something fancier, but Dad said he should have something more plain."

"It sounds like he's a good cook."

"He is. And now that he's left home, I'm stuck with Dad's cooking."

Tara laughed.

"Dad said you work in a quilting store. What do you do there?"

"I'm a sales assistant. We sell Amish quilts, and everything someone would need for quilting."

"Do you like sewing?" Avalon asked.

"Yes, I do. How about yourself?"

"Mom and I used to do needlework, embroidery. It was years ago and then we stopped. I can't remember why."

"That sounds nice. It's always more fun to do it with somebody else."

Tara and the others heard Megan's faint giggles.

"Sounds like they're having fun," Redmond said.

"Yes, it sounds like it."

"I hope they're not gonna take too much longer because I'm starving," Avalon said.

Tara giggled because that was exactly what she was thinking.

When Megan and Brandon brought the food out, Megan explained that she was just showing Brandon a different way to make gravy.

"And if no one likes it, it's not my fault," Brandon said as he placed a large platter of lamb and vegetables in the center of the table. He continued, "I was going to put these onto individual plates, but Megan said this is the Amish way, so this is the way we're doing it tonight."

"We say grace before we eat," Redmond said.

"We do too, so just do what you normally do." Tara closed her eyes.

Redmond said a prayer of thanks for the food. Tara was a little surprised and pleased. The *Englisch* families she'd been in hadn't said thanks to God before they ate.

When everyone started to eat, Tara answered a lot of Avalon's questions about the Amish.

When the meal was over, Brandon stood up. "Megan, would you be kind enough to help me with the dessert?"

"I'd be glad to."

Megan and Brandon carried the serving platter and the plates to the kitchen.

"I hope you like dessert, Tara," Avalon said.

"What is it? I like most desserts. No, I'll correct that, I like all of them."

Avalon giggled. "It's fruit salad, chocolate mousse and ice cream.

"I love all those things."

"Brandon made the ice cream and he made the chocolate mousse. I cut up the fruit salad."

"It sounds delicious."

Tara didn't feel as awkward as she had thought she might. These people were friendly and lovely and nothing like the family she thought she might have come from.

CHAPTER 16

Ask, and it shall be given you; seek, and ye shall find;
knock, and it shall be opened unto you:
Matthew 7:7

REDMOND HAD BEEN WAITING all night to ask Tara some important questions and now he was nearing the Grabers' house, taking Tara and Megan back home. Time was running out.

"I hope you've both had a good night."

"We have. I'm so glad to have met Brandon and Avalon."

"I hope you'll stay in our lives."

Tara nodded.

He pulled into the Grabers' driveway. When he

stopped the car, he said, "Do you mind if I have a word with you in private?"

Megan opened the car door. "I'll leave the two of you to talk. Thanks for tonight and thanks for the ride home, Redmond."

"You're most welcome, Megan."

When they were alone, Tara said, "Do you want to talk here or do you want to come inside the house?"

"Here will be fine. Tara, I own a printing company and if you'd like, I could train you. You could come and work in the family business."

"Really?"

"Yes. You're welcome to come and live at the house too. I just didn't want to overwhelm you, but I want you to know that our home is your home. That's the way it should've been."

"Thank you. What would I do if I worked for you? I don't know anything about printing."

"There are a lot of different jobs you could do and you could be trained for any one of them."

"Really?"

He looked into her eyes and was reminded again of an old photo of his mother. He'd have to find it to show Tara. "Yes, really."

"I don't know what to say."

"It's a big decision. It would bring you closer into our family, but it has to be what's right for you. I've been reading up on the Amish and I'm guessing you consider them to be your family."

Tara nodded. "Can I think about it?"

"Take all the time you need."

"I like having this photo of my mother, and seeing what she looked like from all the other photos."

"I hope you're not mad at her for putting you up for adoption. Knowing Marjorie as I did, I know it couldn't have been an easy thing for her to do. She was the kind of woman who always put herself last even though she was a spitfire on other occasions."

"I'm not mad at her. I'm glad I found out the truth and got to meet you, and Brandon, and Avalon. Avalon is a lot like me."

"Yes. You two got along well. Would you consider coming to dinner once a week?"

Tara nodded. "I think that would be okay. Yes, I'd like that. Can you drive me somewhere else? I'm staying at a friend's house while she's away. It's not far from here."

"Yes, of course."

"Good. Can you give me a minute and I'll just let the Grabers know you're driving me back there tonight?"

"Yes. I'll wait here." Redmond watched Tara walk into the house. He hoped he wasn't rushing the relationship or moving too fast. It was hard to know what to do. There was no guidebook for something like this —no set of rules or unspoken etiquette. He couldn't make up for her past, but he hoped with his support and friendship he could make Tara's future the best it could be. Realizing that the best thing for her might be for him to fade into the background so she could continue with her Amish life, he had to let her take the lead.

She opened the door and got back into the front seat. "Okay."

"All set?"

"Yes." After Tara had given him directions, she explained that she was staying at Elizabeth's house.

"And I understand that Amish people marry young?"

"Compared to other people, I guess. I don't really consider myself Amish. Well, I do in a sense because that's the way I was raised for the last few years. To be officially Amish, you need to be baptized and young people normally do that just before they marry. Before that, young people can go in and out of the community, but not too much."

"Yes, I've read about the *rumspringa.* Do you have a young man you're fond of?"

"I did once. Not so long ago. It's kind of complicated."

He laughed. "Many relationships are. Marjorie and I disagreed on most things, and once we realized we were never going to agree on anything, we worked around it in our own way."

"I want a relationship I don't have to work on."

Redmond laughed. "I hope you get that."

"Me too, or I shall not get married."

Redmond gave Tara a sideways glance. She

reminded him so much of himself and at other times, his wife.

"Take a left here."

He took the left fork in the road and then Tara directed him up a driveway to an old house. "It's in darkness. Do you want me to come in with you?"

"*Nee.* I'll be fine. I've got a lantern right inside the doorway."

"I'll leave my headlights on for you until I see some light in the house."

"Okay. Goodbye, and thanks for tonight."

"Thank you, Tara. And don't forget next Tuesday night. I'll collect you from the Grabers, and Megan too if she wants to come back."

"I'll be waiting. I think Megan will, too." She leaned over and gave him a quick hug before she left the car.

He wiped a tear from his eye as he watched her walk to the front door of the house. That was his daughter, and other people had raised her.

I can't do anything about that now. I must look to the future and not the past, or I'll drive myself mad.

When a light beamed from within the house, he turned the car around and headed down the driveway.

CHAPTER 17

I am not ashamed: for I know whom I have believed, and am persuaded that he is able to keep that which I have committed unto him against that day.
2 Timothy 1:12

TARA WAS IN BED, but hadn't been home long when she heard hoofbeats. Looking out the window, she saw nothing but darkness. She lit the lantern by her bed and carried it as she walked downstairs to see who it was.

As soon as she opened the door, she heard Elizabeth's voice.

"What are you doing home? I thought you'd be at least another two weeks away."

"We got homesick."

"I could go back to Gretchen's if you want to stay here by yourselves tonight."

Elizabeth shook her head. *"Nee.* We can all stay tonight. I need to catch up with what's been happening since I've been gone."

"I'll put on a pot of tea," Tara said, pulling Elizabeth toward the kitchen.

While Joseph unloaded the buggy, the two girls sat in the kitchen drinking tea.

"So much has happened, and all I wanted to do was to talk to you about it."

"Tell me."

"My father—my actual real father—came looking for me. I've met him. I have a younger sister and an older half brother. Megan came with me to meet them just tonight. I've only just got back from his place."

"I can't believe it. I wish I'd been here."

"Me too, and days before that, my father, I just call him Redmond, came to the house and that's where I met him for the very first time with William, Gretchen and Megan." Tara told Elizabeth everything about her family, how her mother had given her away and then gotten back with her father.

"That's amazing. And he never knew about you?"

"No, not until he found the adoption papers after my mother died." Tara jumped up then and got the photo that she'd been given. "This is my mother holding me as a baby. She'd kept it all that time."

"She never forgot you."

"She didn't."

"I'm so happy for you, Tara."

"I've got more news. Mark's back. Did you know?"

"*Nee.* How would I?"

Tara sniggered. "Well, he made up a story about Joseph giving him work to do in the *haus.* Then he confessed it was a lie and he just wanted to spend time with me."

"You're back together with him?"

"*Nee.* Everything is messed up. There are rumors about him."

"There are rumors about everyone. That's not unusual."

"Yeah. Tell me about your visiting?"

"I've been visiting all of Joseph's relations. And staying not more than a night at each place. It's been exhausting; I'm glad I'm home."

"I'm glad you're home, too. We've all missed you."

"There's nothing else to tell. We visit the homes of people, and then we can't relax because we're not in our own home. I felt tense the whole time. That's why we cut it short."

Tara blurted out everything about Mark and what had happened between them. She kept quiet about Caleb, as he was now Elizabeth's brand new brother-in-law.

When Joseph walked into the kitchen, he said, "Do I get a cup of tea?"

Tara sprang to her feet. "Yeah. Take a seat."

He pulled out a chair and sat down. "That's everything out of the buggy. I've just left the boxes in the living room by the door."

"That'll give me plenty to do tomorrow," Elizabeth said. "Tara's had some exciting news." Elizabeth told Joseph about how Tara's father had found her.

"That's good news, Tara."

"I know. It's answered questions I've always had. Now, about those boxes, Elizabeth. I can help you with your unpacking after work, and then can you drive me back home, Joseph?"

"Sure, but don't feel you have to rush off. We said you could stay here for a while. We don't want to ruin your plans."

Tara could scarcely keep the smile from her face. As newlyweds, they'd surely want their new home to themselves. "I have had a good time being on my own. *Denke.* Now I'm ready to go home."

"Okay."

"Tara, I'm going to have a big dinner here and invite everyone."

"When?"

"In about a week."

"Sounds like fun."

"I hope so. All our friends can come take a look at

our new place. We won't have everything done by then, though."

"It'll take some time to get it into the shape we want."

"I'll help you with the dinner."

"*Denke.* I was hoping you would."

"I don't see a buggy here, Tara, has Caleb been driving you?"

Tara frowned as she placed a cup of hot tea in front of Joseph. "Caleb?"

"He drove you here, didn't he?"

"*Jah,* he did. He drove me to work and back a couple of times."

"That's good."

"Did you ask him to?"

"*Nee.*"

"Did you know Mark is back?" Elizabeth asked Joseph.

"*Nee.*" He looked at Tara. "Back to stay?"

Tara shrugged her shoulders. "He can do whatever he wants. It makes no difference to me."

Joseph looked at Elizabeth with raised eyebrows as he picked up his teacup.

Tara guessed that Elizabeth would tell Joseph everything when they were alone. How nice it would be to have someone to confide in.

"You two must be tired."

"*Jah,*" Elizabeth said.

"We're exhausted," Joseph agreed.

"I'll be gone early in the morning. I start early and finish early tomorrow."

"Can I drive you to work?" Joseph asked.

"Nee. I'll get a taxi. It's no trouble."

"Are you sure?"

"Quite sure."

"If I'm awake I'll drive you."

"Forget it. You have a good sleep-in. And then I'll come back and help Elizabeth unpack and then you can drive me back home. Okay?"

He nodded. "Okay."

Tara drank her tea quickly and went to bed feeling like she was an intruder. The least she could do was give them time alone. The first night as a married couple in their new home, and they had Tara under their roof. It wasn't ideal for them and if she'd had her own buggy, she would've gone back home right then.

"GRETCHEN, can I talk to you about something in private?"

"Of course come with me to the barn. I'm getting the chicken food."

Gretchen walked out the door with Tara. "What's on your mind?"

It wasn't easy for Tara to talk to Gretchen about men. They'd had so few talks about them, and any conversations that Gretchen had with the girls about men were in general and not about any man or any relationship in particular. "I'm confused. At first, I liked Mark and, I didn't tell you, but we had discussed marriage and then he disappeared and I don't know where he went."

"Yoder or Hostetler?"

"What?"

"Mark Yoder or Mark Hostetler?"

"Mark Young."

Gretchen raised her eyebrows and said nothing.

"And then he came back with an attitude that it was my problem that he disappeared. And..."

"Did you say that?"

"*Nee,* but whenever we discuss anything, I always end up feeling that it's my problem. He said he wanted to get back together and I said no because I can't trust him and he said it's because I was given away as a child and I have a fear of abandonment or something like that."

"Are you having a problem forgiving him for going away?"

Tara shrugged her shoulders. "I guess he can do whatever he wants, but I just think he's untrustworthy now."

"Well, it might be a good thing that he disappeared when he did."

Tara was suddenly glad that she was talking to Gretchen; things just seem to make sense when they came out of Gretchen's mouth.

"But there is someone else I like."

"That's good."

"I thought it was good to start with, but now I hear that he might not be very trustworthy."

"You don't want to go on what you hear. You need to take people as you find them. There's far too much talk that goes on in the community. Some people have nothing better to do than to gossip."

"It wasn't like that, though, Aunt Gretchen. This person who warned me about him was a very reliable person."

"The bishop?"

Tara nodded. "And that's not all. There are rumors about Mark and Mary Lou. So even if I forgave him for that... I don't know; it just seems that he's far too friendly with Mary Lou for my liking."

"It's interesting that you're so upset about Mark being friendly with Mary Lou. It sounds like you haven't gotten over him."

"I still like him, but I can't trust him."

"Sensible girl. You're choosing a man with your head and your heart. And—"

"So far I'm not choosing one, I'm just unchoosing them, it seems."

Gretchen giggled. "How can I help you?"

"This other boy I like—well, how do I know if the things I've heard about him are true?"

"Why don't you ask him?"

Tara stared into Gretchen's wise face. "Aunt

Gretchen, you're a genius. I never thought of that. I just hope I don't offend him when I ask him."

"You might, but at least then you'll be closer to the truth. You've always been bold and forthright—some might say strong minded—in the past. That's got you into a lot of trouble, but now I see that you are using those emotions and your personality in a good way."

Tara brightened up. "Do you think so?"

"Just ask the young man if what you've heard is true."

Tara looked into Gretchen's kindly face, and wondered if she would have ever had a conversation like that with her birth mother, had things been different.

CHAPTER 18

Knowing that whatsoever good thing any man doeth, the
same shall he receive of the Lord, whether he be bond or free.
Ephesians 6:8

TARA WAS at Elizabeth's big dinner at her house when she next came into contact with Caleb. It was after the dinner was over, and Caleb was getting a breath of fresh air on the porch. She came up behind him as he was staring into the darkness of the night.

"Caleb, can I ask you a question?"

He jumped slightly and then turned to face her. "You can ask me whatever you want."

Tara licked her lips. "If I ask you a question will you answer me truthfully?"

He frowned. "Of course I will."

147

"When you drove me home from the wedding the other day, why did you take me the long way?"

He looked away from her. "I just wanted to spend more time with you."

"And you didn't know that the wheel would come off and we could've been stuck on a deserted road?"

His mouth opened in shock. *"Nee!* How would I know that?"

She could tell by the way he looked into her eyes he was telling the truth. Caleb hadn't plotted for them to be alone and stranded.

"Tara, what's this about?"

"I don't know." She shrugged her shoulders. "Someone just told me to be wary of wolves in sheep's clothing and I guess I'm anxious about everybody around me now."

"You don't have to worry about me. Whoever told you that... I'm sure they had somebody else in mind. Or, did they mention me by name?"

"Nee, they didn't. I'm sorry I said anything."

"I know you don't know me very well, but I hope you'll come to trust me in time."

"It's hard sometimes to trust." She stepped closer to him.

"It can't have been easy for you going from house-to-house like you did when you were younger."

"It wasn't easy at all. I suppose that's how I came to be mistrusting of people."

"You don't have to mistrust me. I only want the best

for you and I have no bad intentions toward you. It was a silly thing for me to do—to go the long way. I should've told you, or I should've asked you if you wanted to go that way home." His voice trailed away.

She wanted to get to know him better. The more layers she peeled away, the better she liked this man. He was like a mystery package.

Feeling that she now knew him well enough, she asked, "How did you get that scar on your face and the scars on your hands?"

His hand flew to his temple where the scar ran down past his eye. It was clear that whatever had caused the deep cut, it had narrowly missed his eye. "These scars are ugly. I wish no one had to look at them."

"*Nee*, they're not ugly. They give you character."

He laughed.

"Will you tell me how you got them?"

He swallowed noticeably. "I had a disagreement with a barbed wire fence."

Tara frowned. "How did it come about?"

"It's a long story."

"I'd like to hear it. I'm intrigued now."

"It happened when I was around eight. It was a Sunday and I wasn't feeling well, so I stayed home with my *grossmammi* while the rest of the family went to the meeting. When we were alone, she started gasping and was having trouble breathing."

"You said you were eight?"

"Thereabouts. I knew I had to go for help, but my family had filled two buggies to go to the meeting, so there was only one horse in the paddock. I was to find out later he wasn't broken under saddle. I slipped a bridle on him and he was fine—didn't flinch or anything. Then I leaped on his back as I often did with our other two horses, and he was sidestepping and wouldn't move forward. Then we hit the fence and he bucked me off into it."

"Oh no." Tara cringed.

"Yeah, and I hung on to him for everything I was worth and was dragged a few paces."

"Ouch."

He looked down at the back of his hands.

"What happened to your grandmother?"

"I'm getting to that. I told you it was a long story. The horse stopped and I got back on him and was able to ride him to the doctor's house."

"How could you get on his back if you were only eight?"

"We used to ride our other horses and learned to vault onto them somehow. We'd take a handful of mane and jump just right and up we'd go. Anyway, when I arrived at the doctor's house, I had blood all over me and he thought I'd come there for myself. I told him about my *grossmammi* and then he drove me back and found she was having an asthma attack. He was able to treat her."

"You saved her life."

He sniggered. "I think that's an exaggeration."

"I don't. Did you need stitches for your cuts?"

"*Nee.* I was bandaged up and that was that. Apart from some injections for tetanus and probably some kind of antibiotic."

"What about your face?"

"Believe it or not, I had it bandaged too." He laughed. "I wasn't allowed to move for days. I had large cotton swathes out to here." He motioned with his hand. "I can laugh about it now, but it was pretty awful."

Tara grimaced imagining the pain. "That was so brave of you to go for help, and you were so young."

"Anyone would do it."

With a loud guttural clearing of his throat, Mark stepped onto the porch.

They both turned around and looked at him.

"Tara, could I have a private word with you?" He looked over at Caleb. "I'm sorry Caleb, but I need to speak with Tara."

"Okay." He stepped down the porch steps and walked into the dark yard.

Mark walked over and stood next to her. "I thought I'd do you a favor and save you from him. You looked bored."

"That's clever of you to be able to see that from the back of my head."

"Don't be sarcastic. It doesn't suit you. Anyone would be bored with Caleb."

"I don't think you know him very well."

"Does anyone?"

Tara blew out a deep breath. "What did you want to speak with me about?"

"Marry me?"

"We've talked about this."

"We'll have to keep talking about it until you say yes."

"What will Mary Lou think if you marry me?"

"She'll think that you're very blessed to have a man like me as your future husband."

"I'll ask her and see if that's true."

His face instantly went stiff. "Why would you talk to her about me?"

"I've heard a lot about you and Mary Lou lately and I've seen you talking with her on a number of occasions." It was only two, but that didn't sound as good.

"I don't like the way you're talking now, Tara. What's gotten into you? I liked you better the way you were before."

"I could leave and go away, too, all of a sudden."

"Where would you go?"

From the look on his face, he thought she was serious. Tara had to think fast. "I've just met my family. I could leave the community and go to live with them. They've invited me."

"Would you?"

"I might."

"That would work out perfectly for both us. Now I

can tell you that when I was away, I was looking into becoming a mechanic and working on cars. We could build a life away from the community."

Tara jerked her head back and stared at him. The bishop had been giving her hints to be wary of Mark and not Caleb.

CHAPTER 19

*For we wrestle not against flesh and blood, but against
principalities, against powers, against the rulers of the
darkness of this world,
against spiritual wickedness in high places.*
Ephesians 6:12

"My place is not with you, Mark. I thought it might
have been, once."

"You won't do better than me, Tara. I could have
any woman I want and I'm not saying that because I'm
being prideful."

"Then you must not waste your time on me." Tara
walked down the lightly snow-covered porch steps.

"Tara, where are you going?"

Tara hurried off into the darkness hoping Mark wouldn't follow. When she walked around the barn, she looked around for Caleb, convinced that was the direction he'd gone. Just when she was about to turn back, there was movement to the left of her.

"Caleb?"

He strode toward her. "What are you doing out in the dark like this?"

"Looking for you."

He glanced back at the house. "You finished with Mark?"

"Yes, finally, all finished with him. I was through with him days ago, but I've finally convinced him we're never getting back together."

"I meant finished speaking with him just now," Caleb said smiling.

"Oh." She shook her head and looked down. "I'm such an idiot, I thought… never mind."

"What did you think? That I'd like to know you and Mark were over with and your secret relationship no longer exists?"

"Something like that. I guess it wasn't so secret, though." She looked into his eyes. "You're happy it's over with Mark?"

"It's the best news I've heard since I can't remember when."

She laughed and wasn't certain what to say, which was unusual for her.

"If you were my girlfriend, I wouldn't keep something like that a secret. I couldn't. I'd have to tell everyone."

"You would?"

"Jah. I'd want everyone to know."

"And what else?"

"I would ask you to marry me, and then marry you real quick if you said yes, before you could change your mind."

Just as Tara laughed, the wind picked up and a chilly gust of wind smacked the ends of her prayer *kapp* strings across her face.

Gently, he pulled them away from her face and tucked them into the sides of her prayer *kapp.* Her heart pounded at his closeness and his soft touch.

"Tara," he breathed. "Would you like to do something together, just the two of us?"

Nodding, she replied, "I'd like that."

"You would?"

"Jah."

"Okay. How about I come to collect you at six tomorrow night and we'll have dinner somewhere?"

"Perfect." Tara glanced back at the house and saw Elizabeth standing on the porch and guessed she was looking for the two of them. "I guess we should get back."

"I suppose we should, although I'd much rather stand here talking to you in the moonlight."

She looked up into his face and wanted to kiss him right there, right then. He took hold of her hand and gently brought it to his lips and kissed it. Waves of happiness tingled through her body and she knew that this was the man she'd someday marry.

"Let's go inside and not leave each other's side until the night is over. We'll let the gossips say what they will," he said. "We can ignore the whispers and the raised eyebrows."

"All right. Let's do it, but if Mark tells you to leave again, I won't let you go."

He chuckled. "Okay. I'll stay by you."

They walked back to the house side by side.

Throughout the night, Tara could see that Mark was fuming. He wasn't a fool, and he knew that something was happening between her and Caleb. Thankfully, Mark didn't have anything to say, and he left with the others when it was time to go home.

Tara said goodnight to Elizabeth and Joseph before she walked outside with Megan. Tara hurried over to Caleb who was just about to leave.

"I'll see you tomorrow night, Caleb."

"I'm looking forward to it."

When he drove away, she walked back to the porch to wait with Megan for Aunt Gretchen and Uncle William.

"So, it's Caleb now?"

"Is it so obvious?"

"Jah."

Tara giggled. "He's so honest and he's got nothing to hide."

"Jah, he's nice. I like him. What about what the bishop said?"

"I found out tonight that he wasn't talking about Caleb."

"That's good. Maybe you can take Caleb to dinner with your family on Tuesday night next week?"

"Well, maybe not that soon, but I'd reckon he'll be going there with me shortly." Tara stared at his buggy lights as they disappeared into the darkness. She wished the night had gone on longer so she could have spent more time with him.

Megan waved a hand in front of Tara's face, causing Tara to look at her.

Megan laughed. "You're a goner."

"A goner?"

"You've fallen hard for him. I can see it on your face. You were never like this when you were secretly dating Mark."

"Speaking of that, what about you and Brandon?"

"What do you mean?"

Tara nudged Megan with her elbow. "Aw c'mon. I've never seen you talk like that with any man. I'm surprised you don't want to keep going there every Tuesday with me."

Megan's lips twisted upward at the corners. "We've been talking other than Tuesday nights. He gave me his phone number. He's not Amish, but I wasn't born Amish either."

Tara resisted giving Megan any cautions. It was up to her to decide her own future.

It was four weeks later that Caleb went with Tara to meet her birth family. After Redmond drove them back to the Grabers after dinner, William, Gretchen and Megan had made themselves scarce, giving Tara and Caleb some time alone.

"We must be late getting back," Caleb said when he saw that no one was around.

Tara whispered, "I think they're leaving us alone."

"Oh. Good idea."

"Sit with me," Tara sat on the couch and Caleb sat right beside her.

"*Denke* for taking me there with you tonight. I'm glad you're letting me into your world."

Tara giggled and took hold of his hand. "You let me into yours."

"My life has an open door and yours is closed."

"You weren't so easy to get to know."

He pulled back and stared at her. "What do you mean?"

"That first time you drove me out to Elizabeth and Joseph's house you didn't say a word."

"I did too."

"Barely. Maybe you grunted once or twice."

Caleb laughed. "I guess you're right. I don't feel

comfortable with a lot of people, which leads me to my next suggestion."

"What's that?"

"That we marry."

Tara smiled and looked into his eyes. "I want to marry you, but not right now. Can we wait?"

"For what?"

"I'm adjusting to what I found out about my past and who I am." She waved her hand around her head. "My head's in a muddle."

He grabbed her hand in mid air and lowered it and kept a hold of it. "I don't care if it's next week or next year just give me a proper answer, and you must mean it with all your heart." Caleb looked into her eyes, "Tara, will you marry me?"

"Depends."

"On what?"

"Do you have any interest in cars?"

Frowning, he asked, "Cars?"

She nodded.

He grimaced. *"Nee.* I don't."

"Would you ever leave the community?"

After a silent moment, he answered, "Only if you wanted to leave."

"Really? You'd leave with me?"

"I'd leave reluctantly, but someone has to look after you. Are you thinking of leaving?"

"Nee."

He swallowed hard. "Tara, we've spoken of these things before."

"I know. I'm just making sure I can give you an honest answer to your question."

With a slight squeeze of her hand, he said, "Don't keep a man waiting."

"Come closer and let me whisper my answer." He leaned his head closer to hers, and she whispered, "Yes. I will marry you, Caleb."

Tara now had everything she wanted. She'd learned about and come to terms with her past. Her past had brought her two siblings and a father. Her future came with a man she could trust. Caleb wasn't the best looking man in the community, but he possessed all the qualities that were important to her in a man and more. He'd stand by her, never leave her, and he was open and honest.

A smile spread across Caleb's face after he'd heard the words he'd longed for Tara to say. He turned to face her and their lips met in their very first kiss.

Blessed is the man that endureth temptation: for when he is tried, he shall receive the crown of life, which the Lord hath promised to them that love him.
James 1:12

Thank you for your interest in *Amish Foster Girl.*
The next book in the series is,
The New Amish Girl.

ABOUT THE AUTHOR

Samantha Price is a best selling author who knew she wanted to become a writer at the age of seven, while her grandmother read to her Peter Rabbit in the sun room. Though the adventures of Peter and his sisters Flopsy, Mopsy, and Cotton-tail started Samantha on her creative journey, it is now her love of Amish culture that inspires her to write. Her writing is clean and wholesome, with more than a dash of sweetness. Though she has penned over eighty Amish Romance and Amish Mystery books, Samantha is just as in love today with exploring the spiritual and emotional journeys of her characters as she was the day she first put pen to paper. Samantha lives in a quaint Victorian cottage with three rambunctious dogs.

www.samanthapriceauthor.com
    samanthaprice333@gmail.com
    www.facebook.com/SamanthaPriceAuthor
    Follow Samantha Price on BookBub
    Twitter @ AmishRomance

Made in the USA
Lexington, KY
16 February 2018